THE AGE OF TERROR

THE AGE OF TERROR

David Plante

ST. MARTIN'S PRESS ❧ NEW YORK

The photograph "The corpse of Zoya Kosmodemyanskaya near the grave where she was buried by Hitlerites before the retreat from Petristchevo village," Moscow Region, 1941, is reprinted with the permission of the Museum of Revolution, Moscow, Russia.

Design by Nancy Resnick

Library of Congress Cataloging-in-Publication Data

Plante, David.
    The age of terror : a novel / by David Plante.
        p.   cm.
    ISBN 0-312-19824-8
    I. Title.
PS3566.L257A67   1999
813'.54—dc21   98-42993
                                            CIP

First Edition: January 1999

10   9   8   7   6   5   4   3   2   1

To Mary Gordon
with love

ACKNOWLEDGMENTS

TO ALL MY GOOD FRIENDS FOR THEIR SUPPORT AND especially to Marvin Siegel, and to my editor, Bob Weil, and my agent, Lynn Nesbit, many thanks.

Keep Zoya's photograph beside you always . . .
Her virgin body
        stretched out in snow . . .
The destined lover never came to save her . . .

Margarita Aligher

THE AGE OF TERROR

PREDELLA

WANDERING FROM ROOM TO ROOM ON A HOT SUMMER afternoon as if looking for a room he had never been into, Joe settled on the living room and picked up a magazine with an article about the Soviet Union during World War II. He opened it to this photograph. Shocked, he shut the magazine quickly, but then he sat on a rocking chair and placed it on his knees and rocked back and forth until, with a pang of helplessness, he opened the magazine again and stared at the photograph.

The photograph was of Zoya Kosmodemyanskaya, a Soviet partisan who had fought for her belief in the Soviet Union and was captured and tortured and hanged by the enemy Germans. Looking at it, Joe felt once more the pang come over him with a terrible helplessness.

He closed the magazine and put it down and for a moment remained still, then he went out of the house into the backyard, where there was a clothesline with sheets and pillowcases and shirts hanging, and a wicker laundry basket on the scruffy grass next to a red, slated lawn chair. On three sides of the yard were woods, woods with birch trees leaning across one another and tangled with yellowing wild grapevines, the sunlight shining down through the high, thin-leaved branches, and through the trees shone a lake in sunlight. On the fourth side of the yard was the house—a brown, clapboard house with a fieldstone chimney from which a tangle of honeysuckle hung, and a screened-in back door with a stoop of large, flat stones. By the door was the closed bulkhead into the cellar. Seagulls were flying round high above the roof.

Helpless not to think about it, he thought of that photograph of Zoya Kosmodemyanskaya, and his thinking made him walk back and forth across the grass, along the clothesline. He leaned against one of the wooden posts from which the clothesline, sagging with sheets and shirts, was strung.

He said, "God."

Unable to be still, he walked again along the clothesline to the post at the other end.

Where he would go and what he would do he didn't know. He thought of going to the Holy Land, but he knew at the same time that that would be no help.

Joe walked to the edge of the woods and looked into the trees, some dead, stripped of bark and pale, with broken branches hanging from the trunks.

He didn't know where he would go and what he would do

any more than he knew why such a profound helplessness was roused in him by the photograph of Zoya Kosmodemyanskaya.

Back in the hot, still house, Joe went into the living room to pick up the magazine with the photograph in it, then upstairs to his bedroom. Hanging on the wall over his bed was a crucifix, the contorted Corpus ivory white and the cross ebony black. Joe shut his door and sat on the edge of his bed and studied yet again the photograph of Zoya Kosmodemyanskaya: the way one of her breasts had been cut away to her ribs, the way her neck was elongated and her head twisted by the rope she'd been hanged by, her closed eyes, her ragged hair.

The impulse came to him to get up and kneel on his pillow and lean his forehead against the foot of the cross. But he heard footsteps outside his room, and, with a start, he became rigid.

ONE

Joe expected snow to be falling in Leningrad, but when left off at his hotel, he saw the high sky was clear. Standing in the winter sunlight in the square were tall, slender, beautiful girls who appeared to be wandering about, stopping now and then to chat with one another. They looked at Joe as he passed among them with his suitcase.

The corridor floors of the hotel were covered with linoleum patterned like parquet, with runners over the linoleum. The white wooden doors to the rooms, with the numbers written where the old brass numbers had fallen off, were slightly askew on their hinges. Joe followed a porter in a frayed uniform and with pomaded hair pushing his suitcase on a trolley. A gang of children, five American boys and girls, ran past, calling to one another, "I'll get there first," "No, you won't, I will," "I will," and they giggled.

The porter wheeled the suitcase to a woman sitting behind

a desk, a large but beautiful woman whose face was powdered white and whose long hair was dyed matte black. The porter gave her a card with a number written on it, and in return the woman gave him a key with a big metal ring and a metal tag. Behind her was a glass case of teapots and cups and saucers and metal seltzer bottles.

She said to Joe expressionlessly, "When you leave hotel, bring key to me, I give you hotel pass. Do not lose hotel pass. Without hotel pass, you cannot come back into hotel, you cannot get key. Understand?"

"I understand," Joe said.

He again followed the porter down the long corridor. Joe waited in the vestibule just inside his room for the porter to switch on the lights. He gave a ruble to the porter, who, bowing a little, left. Joe took off his overcoat and scarf and hung them on hooks in the vestibule.

As he entered the room, separated from a sleeping alcove by a green velvet curtain drawn back from a bed with a green velvet cover, the telephone rang. Over the old-fashioned, black receiver a voice spoke in Russian, and Joe, not knowing what to answer, said nothing. The voice paused, waiting, then went on, a man's voice. All Joe could think of to say was *"Pazhalsta,"* which he had learned, along with the Cyrillic alphabet and a few other expressions, before coming to the Soviet Union. He said *please* a number of times in Russian, and after a long, tense silence the man at the other end of the line hung up. The green velvet curtain was worn along its folds, and the gray carpet in the room dusty. A couple of French-style armchairs upholstered in green velvet stood turned away from each other.

Joe threw his clothes on the bed and went into the bathroom. Many of the white tiles on the walls had cracked, and cement covered the patches of missing black-and-white mosaic on the floor. The water that gushed into the huge bathtub when Joe turned on the taps was dark with rust. As he stood in the rusty water to wash himself, he saw, across the bathroom and over the round pedestal washbasin, a mirror and himself in the mirror. He had the sudden sense of his naked body being pulled down, and he held himself against the pull until the feeling passed. He rinsed himself, dried himself with the thin, napless towels, and went into the room to take fresh clothes from his bag and dress.

The telephone rang. Again, that voice spoke in Russian. Joe said, "I'm sorry, I don't understand," and immediately the man hung up.

By lifting the net curtain over the window in his room Joe could see out into a well, and as he looked out snow began to fall in Leningrad.

He kept telling himself he must go out, must at least go out to see again those girls wandering about in the square before the hotel, but it seemed to him that alone he was forbidden to go out, that in the Soviet Union, where so much must be forbidden, certainly going out on his own was. He thought he shouldn't be allowed in the Soviet Union to do anything on his own.

Putting on his scarf, overcoat, his gloves, seemed to require detailed concentration. Dressed, he realized he had to use the toilet. Then, dressed again to go out, he saw he'd forgotten to put on his gloves and he couldn't remember where he'd put them. They were on the bathroom washbasin. Opening the door to leave his room, he paused because he was sure he'd forgotten something, and he went through everything he must have on him to go out in case he was stopped: his passport and visa. Then he remembered: his hotel pass.

But the woman was not at her desk along the corridor. Joe

walked up and down for half an hour and returned to his room, thinking, as he couldn't go out without his pass, he'd stay in. After another half hour he went out again and saw the woman at her station. He handed her the key, the tag of which she examined, then she opened a drawer in the desk and took out a small stack of passes, but she could not find his. Again she examined the number on the tag and again went through the passes but, frowning, didn't find his. She frowned at him.

Joe raised and lowered his shoulders.

"Without pass," she said, "you cannot have key."

In his confusion, Joe laughed, but the woman didn't laugh, not even when, going through the passes once more, she found his.

She frowned more when she handed it to him. "Do not lose."

His confusion made him think he had still forgotten something. As he went past the commissionaire in a uniform and out the hotel through the revolving door, it came to him that he had forgotten something vital, and he stood outside on the snow-cleared sidewalk to try to remember what.

Outside, the snow was driven by a wet, sideward wind. The young, tall, beautiful women, some in cloth coats and some in fur coats, with fur hats and bright silk scarves tight about their throats, were standing, at distances from one another, in that snow. A small group of them were standing before a woman, a little older than they were and wearing a gray woolen scarf, talking to them, and they appeared to listen carefully. The woman talking glanced at Joe as he went out into the square, where there was a huge, black church, half its black dome snow-white.

Even though there was no traffic anywhere in sight, Joe, who thought he must in the Soviet Union obey all the regulations, waited for the light to change before he crossed over into the square. The wind drew Joe a little to one side, then, out where the square was open, the wind drew him to the other side. Only one car, its headlights on, passed close by him.

He walked down the center of a long, narrow park. In the falling snow, he couldn't see beyond the two rows of bare trees. Between the rows was a red stone plinth with the black bust of Gogol, and Joe stopped to study the bust.

He knew that Gogol, in his despair, had gone to the Holy Land for help, but the Holy Land hadn't helped him.

He walked toward a bridge over the Neva, but stopped before crossing. It seemed to him it must not be permitted for him to cross the bridge. No footsteps were in the snow that covered the footpaths along either side. He waited awhile, feeling the wind penetrate his overcoat, then he proceeded along the untrodden footpath to the middle of the black iron bridge and looked over the snow-covered parapet.

Channeled by the wind, the white snow, gathered, it seemed, from the air about him, streamed down in long drifts along with the current of black water on which ice floes bobbed.

Joe drew back from the parapet when he sensed someone walking toward him and turned a little to see a woman in a long suede coat and high-heeled boots and a fur hat and a gray woolen scarf, and he remembered he had seen her talking to the women with the bright scarves outside the hotel.

Quickly, he looked down again, to where the water, separated by one of the breakwaters, folded into a whirlpool as it flowed together just beyond it. Blocks of ice spun in the whirlpool.

He turned again to see that the woman, with a broad, smooth, blond face, made taut, it seemed, by her high cheekbones, was staring at him with dark eyes, her lips parted as if

9

she were about to speak. Her long suede coat was stained, and her boots, of patent leather, were cracked, the fake leather peeling from the heels, and her hat was of yellow cat fur.

Her lips still parted, the woman looked at Joe, then looked beyond him, in the direction from which he had come. He turned, too, to look. A man in a coarse, brown coat and a brown rabbit-fur hat was standing, as if idling, just off the bridge. As Joe looked from him back to the woman, she, frowning as she gave Joe one last look, passed by him. She crossed to the other parapet of the bridge to avoid passing by the man in the brown coat.

Again, Joe stared down into the river. Two long, rough, crossed beams of wood appeared from under the arches of the bridge and, sinking and rising, twisting and turning among the ice floes, were folded away into the swift current.

When Joe glanced to the side, he saw the man in the brown coat still standing there.

Joe followed the woman's footsteps across to the parapet on the other side of the bridge, away from the man, and he continued to follow the footsteps from the bridge. There were no cars, but pedestrians in the square, isolated figures in the falling snow, and soon Joe lost the footsteps of the woman. But he continued across the square to the beginning of the wide Nevsky Prospect, down the center of which only one snow-piled car drove, its lights off, and where huddled pedestrians walked the sidewalks. When the doors to the crowded shops along the Prospect were opened, many boots appeared standing on muddy, slush-covered wooden floors, with string bags hanging among the boots.

Joe heard a loud voice behind him, shouting in Russian, and he thought for a moment he was being shouted at. He turned quickly, and an old, toothless man with a huge hat of tabby-

cat fur was shouting at him in Russian. No one passing stopped
to listen. Joe hunched his shoulders and raised his arm as the
man kept shouting, spittle flying from his lips.

"*Ya nye panemayou*," Joe said, "*ya nye panemayou.*" He didn't
understand.

He heard laughter behind him, a woman's throaty laughter,
and turned round to a woman who said, "He is shouting at
you for not wearing hat."

She was the woman he had encountered on the bridge over
the Neva, and Joe immediately thought, She has followed me.

She spoke in Russian to the old man, who, frowning severely
at Joe, pointed to his own hat and continued to shout, but the
woman, laughing as she spoke more to the old man, silenced
him, and still frowning severely, he left. She said to Joe, "You
will be stopped often by old people and reprimanded for not
wearing hat. You will catch bad cold."

Joe put his gloved hands to his hair, which was thick with
snow. "I'm sure they're right."

"You don't have hat?"

"No."

"You must get hat."

They were standing where pedestrians passed them on both
sides. Two naval cadets, the skirts of their black greatcoats
swinging, passed on one side in one direction, and an old
woman, with a string bag bulging with newspaper-wrapped
bundles, passed in the other direction.

Joe thought the woman standing before him was going to
say something more about—as Russians often dropped the articles—hat, but she, her dark eyes narrowed, stared past him
in such a way that he looked round. Standing at a corner was
the man in the brown coat.

The woman said to Joe, "So you are still being followed."

"Why?"

The woman laughed her throaty laugh, the laugh of an older woman, though she was not old, but young. She blinked from the snow flying about her face. She said, "He himself probably doesn't know why."

The man glanced away.

Suddenly taking Joe's arm, the woman said, "Shall we give him fun? Shall we walk together and make him wonder? He is bored, I know he must be bored. Let us give him little fun."

She drew Joe with her in the direction from which he'd come, holding his arm closely, and he went with her.

She said with a slight warble in her voice, though she held her chin up, "Here I am, taking risk of walking and talking with foreigner in street." Joe felt her grasp his arm a little more tightly. She laughed. "And do I care?"

"Do you?"

"No, I do not care. Isn't that amazing, that I don't care? If you are not amazed, I am amazed."

"Will he arrest us?"

She threw her head back when she laughed so her long, slender throat showed above her gray woolen scarf folded under the greasy collar of her coat. With her, Joe suddenly felt a free forward movement in whatever direction she was headed.

And he had the very curious feeling of having walked together down the Nevsky Prospect with her many times before, though he had never before walked down the Nevsky Prospect and certainly not with her; and, as if in the past, of having joked with her whenever he and she were together walking down the Nevsky Prospect.

She said, "When we stop at the next corner, you glance back to see if he is following us."

Joe glanced back. The man was a block behind, and when

he saw Joe turn, he immediately went to look into a shop window, though there was nothing in the window.

"He's there."

"Now where shall we go that will make him really wonder?"

Joe wondered if she had in fact been following him, and if she and the man now following them both were working together.

On the other side of the side street, he asked, "Are you taking a risk walking with me?"

"I hope."

"But why?"

"Because, when I saw you on bridge and recognized you as American standing there, all alone, looking down at river, I wondered, what kind of American can this be, here, alone, standing on bridge? And I wanted to go to you and ask. But when I saw KGB man, I left. Then, when I saw you again just now, being shouted at just like any Russian for not wearing hat, I decided, KGB man or not, I will risk doing what I would never have done before."

"What is happening?"

"Oh, everything. Soon, everything will be possible in Soviet Union. Soon, there will be possible what we could never have imagined even a year ago. It will happen very, very quickly."

"Have I come to the Soviet Union at the right or wrong time, then?"

"That depends on what you want. You will be able to do in Soviet Union what you would never be able to do in United States." She laughed her throaty laugh. "And because that will be terrible, I must hope that KGB man will arrest me."

Joe, too, laughed. "To really excite the KGB man, we could go to my hotel."

"That would be big risk."

"Too big?"

"If I am going to take risk, it should be the biggest possible. Where is your hotel?"

"The Astoria."

"We shall see if they let me in."

"Why shouldn't they let you in if I, a guest, ask you?"

"You are foreigner, I am Soviet citizen, and you have more rights in Soviet Union than I do. I am not allowed in hotel where foreigners stay. Or, since I last tried, I was not. We shall see now. But look to see if KGB man is still behind us."

"He is."

"This will be real fun. We shall do this—when we enter hotel, I will hold your arm as you show your hotel pass and we will go past commissionaire quickly. He will think I prostitute with you."

As they passed among the tall, thin women with their bright scarves about their throats still standing outside the hotel, Joe suddenly thought, They are of course prostitutes.

He imagined that they smiled a little at the woman on his arm as he and she walked among them, but the woman, who had just a little while before been talking to them, didn't even glance at them, but held Joe's arm more tightly.

As she and Joe went through the revolving doors of the hotel, the commissionaire, in a frayed uniform greasy around the stand-up collar, turned away.

The woman said, "I see now that Soviet Union really is breaking apart. They do not look at who enters hotel. This is terrible. Should I go tell commissionaire he is not doing his duty as Soviet citizen?"

Outside the revolving glass doors, the man in the long brown coat and brown fur hat was standing in the falling snow among the prostitutes.

Joe said, "The KGB man still seems to be doing his duty."

"Then, perhaps, there is still some hope. But we shall see if he waits until we leave."

They deposited their coats in the cloakroom, where the young woman, after removing her fur hat, stood at a mirror and ran her fingers through her long, light, loose hair. She was wearing a black angora sweater and a black woolen skirt. As she once again took Joe's arm, he felt her body heat. She guided him to the only restaurant open in the hotel, one of many old, once grand but now run-down restaurants, in a winter garden, where all there was to order was black bread and butter and caviar and tea.

The young woman asked, "But there is always champagne. Shall we have champagne?"

Joe called the waiter back and ordered a bottle of champagne.

Alone in the large restaurant, they clinked their frothing flutes.

The woman said, swinging her hair, "I am Zoya."

She did not, she said, live in Petersburg, but in Moscow, and was only in Petersburg for three days.

"You say Petersburg and not Leningrad?" Joe asked.

She smiled and asked his name.

"I'm Joe."

"Such an American name. To think, the first time I am speaking to foreigner is with American with the so American name of Joe." Holding her champagne flute high, she looked at Joe over it. "Tell me, Joe, why you are in Soviet Union? To see it break apart so much that Soviets can go into hotels where foreigners stay and drink champagne with them?"

Joe simply smiled a wide smile.

"So you don't want to tell me. Very well, don't tell me. I am used to not knowing why people do what they do."

Joe blushed a little as his smile became wider, showing even, strong teeth in a mouth with large, dark lips.

Zoya drank down her champagne. Then, with a swing of her arm, she poured more into her flute, laughed, and said, "Tell me, Joe, when you were standing on bridge, were you thinking of jumping into river?"

"What made you think that?"

"Maybe it is because I am Russian that I thought it."

"Do Russians always think of jumping into a river when they stand on a bridge and look down into it?"

"Always. There is no other reason for Russian to stand on bridge and look down into river than to jump into it."

"And do they jump?"

"They jump, they jump. I had aunt who went every day to bridge to stare down into Moscow River, day after day, waiting for her exit visa to go to America. She had made up her mind that if she was refused her exit visa, she would jump into river, and she went every day to prepare herself. Either America or river."

"And what happened?"

"She jumped into river."

"She had no other choice?"

"For her, no, she had no other choice." Zoya laughed. "Don't be sad. Maybe she made the better choice." She tilted the bottle to see how much champagne was left in it, then filled Joe's flute and poured the remainder into hers. "So, tell me, when you were looking down into river, you were thinking you wanted to jump?"

Laughing, Joe said, "Do you think I came to Russia for that?"

"Is possible."

Joe laughed more, and he saw in Zoya's eyes that she had, after having thought about it, formed an image of him—though he was twenty-three, she saw him as a boy of thirteen.

Her dark eyes, with lashes black with mascara, concentrated on him, she smiled and said, "Or is possible you came to Russia for other reason."

"It's possible."

"Russians always suspect there are other reasons for a person doing something than what the person says."

"What do you think my reason is, then?"

Zoya raised her chin so her long, slender neck elongated, and she said with a slight thrill that implied a friendly warning in it, "I shall find it out."

"Maybe I came to Russia to meet someone."

"As I want to go to America to meet someone."

"Then you should go and meet him."

Zoya laughed, a rough laugh. "Go to America? Go to USA as easily as you come to USSR?"

"You can't go?"

Zoya shrugged a shoulder. "Now, exit visas are easy to get. Maybe Soviet Union thinks solution to our problems is for everyone to leave, everyone, so there will be nothing, nothing left but our great forests under snow. But now entry visas into Western countries are difficult to get, because Western countries do not want problems of millions of Soviets. What would America do with millions of Soviets with worthless rubles even Russian taxi drivers will not accept in payment, and no hard currency? Entry visa to America is for Russian very difficult, very. But I would so like to go to America to meet someone."

That sense of having known her before, of her being in some way familiar to him, came back to Joe, and he studied her face.

She, smiling, let him study it as if she were used to people studying her face. But, he thought, how could a face that seemed so familiar to him seem also so strange?

They were the only people in the restaurant, and when, after a long while, the tea and the bread and butter and the tiny glass bowl of black caviar arrived, Joe and Zoya became silent, as if to try to talk more would leave them with no possible reason for being together. When Joe, who began to make small, awkward gestures, let the knife slip out of his fingers when he was buttering his bread, Zoya said quietly, "Be careful." And he tried to be careful.

He ordered another bottle of champagne.

As he poured some out, Joe had more distinctly than before the feeling that Zoya saw him as a boy; a boy who, with her, gave her all the attention in the world, but a boy who, mostly alone, was frightened to be alone.

When the second bottle was empty, Zoya laughed a deep, loud laugh, Joe wasn't sure about what.

She said, "Let us go see, now, if our KGB man is still waiting. I shall be very worried if he is not, because that will mean our Soviet Union has lost all its values, all."

In the cloakroom, Joe helped Zoya on with her suede coat, the lining of which, he noted, was torn.

She stood for a moment before him and stared at him.

"What's the matter?" he asked.

"Your hat. You must have hat."

"Where can I get one?"

"Hotel hard-currency shop will have hats, I know."

Zoya, who had made Joe think she'd never before been in this hotel, knew just how to get to the hard-currency shop of the hotel, where, among the shelves of bottles of vodka and whiskey, she made Joe try on one hat after another until she,

clapping her hands together and laughing, said, "Yes, this one."
He looked at himself in a mirror: a young man with a pale,
square face with a black stubble of beard no matter how closely
he shaved and black eyebrows that almost met over the bridge
of his nose. He had large, wet, black eyes, and wide, dark lips.
The fur hat with long hairs stuck out in a wide circle about his
head was also black. In the mirror he saw reflected Zoya's smiling face.

She said, "Now no one will shout at you in street for not
wearing hat."

It was as though she gave him no choice, he must go out
with her; but not having a choice was all right with him, and
he would go anywhere with her.

The snow had stopped, but the low sky was dark. The KGB
man had removed himself from the prostitutes and was leaning
against one of the great pillars of the portico of the cathedral
in the square. When he saw Zoya and Joe come out of the
hotel, he stood away from the pillar.

Zoya said, "I see there are still some who are having fun
trying to sustain Soviet values. I am not disappointed."

"What would they do to us if we were arrested?" Joe asked.

"You would not be arrested. I would be arrested when on
my own. And then I would see what they would do." She
smiled. "I would like to know what, now, happens when a Soviet citizen is arrested. Instead of being sent to labor camp or
psychiatric hospital or to Lubyanka to be shot, what would they
do with me? Maybe they would tell me I must leave our country, and then, what would I do, because I think no other country would have me?" Zoya took Joe's arm. "Let us see what he
will do now."

"Is this really worth the risk?"

"It is worth the risk. Being with American is worth the risk.

Being with American while KGB man follows us is such fun
that it is worth all risk."

"Follows us where?"

"I will show you. We shall make him wonder more about
us. And you shall see Russia."

Her arm in his, Zoya led Joe into side streets, and from time
to time Joe glanced round to see if they were still being followed. They were, though the KGB man hung back at corners.
When passing an open manhole in the snow-covered sidewalk
from which a long, narrow, wooden ladder stuck up, Joe dis-
engaged his arm from Zoya's to stop and look down into the
darkness where he saw the faint beam of a flashlight. Zoya had
gone on ahead of him, and he hurried to catch up to her.

"What were you looking at?" she asked.

He didn't answer, but looked round to see the KGB man
also looking down into the open manhole.

This made Joe laugh to himself: that the KGB man would
examine an open manhole because Joe had stopped to glance
down into it.

Zoya again took Joe's arm as they turned into a fenced-in
churchyard, where, as if in a field of snow, stood a blue-and-
white church. A smell of burning beeswax candles seemed to
penetrate the walls of the church into the cold outside. Zoya,
holding a door open for Joe, said, "Now take off hat," and he
did, entering among low vaults where candles were burning
before icons. People were lined up to buy candles, and others,
with candles in their hands, slowly walked round the crowded
church, murmuring. Most of the people were women with
knitted caps and felt boots.

Joe followed Zoya to the altar screen, where she kissed an
icon and crossed herself three times. To the left, baptisms were

taking place: about a holy-water font, people in a circle, among them girls and boys and very old people carrying candles and mothers and fathers carrying screaming babies, were going round and round, the priest, in a gold-embroidered cope and chanting, going round with them. Some parents tried to shush the screaming, red-faced babies, some let them scream. The chanting of the priest rose above the screaming.

Then, to the right of the altar screen, Joe saw, past the long overcoats and boots of another congregation, three open coffins, and in them the pale, shut faces of women, their noses, chins, cheeks pointed. They appeared to have white kerchiefs folded over their foreheads. Propped against the coffins were flower wreaths with ribbons; candles, in stands, were burning at the foot of each coffin. A woman standing by a coffin reached in and touched the cheek of a dead woman. Zoya went toward this multiple funeral service, and Joe with her. The altar at that side of the church was covered with an oilcloth patterned with daisies, and the priest at the altar was chanting.

Joe suddenly found himself standing next to a woman who was sobbing into a white handkerchief that she held over her nose and mouth.

He pressed his hat to his chest and remained very still. When Zoya said to him, "Come, I will show you more," he didn't move. She asked, "What is wrong?" but, wide-eyed, clutching his hat to his chest and standing tensely still, he didn't answer.

"Joe? Joe?" She held out a hand to him from which she had removed the glove, and he stared at it for a long while before he, with his gloved hand, reached for it, and she led him away.

He turned back to see the woman weeping into a handkerchief.

Zoya led him up old wooden stairs to the upper church, where a mass was being said behind the high altar screen. The church was crowded with people standing. Just when Zoya, still holding his hand, led Joe in, the rococo golden gates of the altar screen were being closed. A large golden sun, attached by one of its rays to the mullion, shook in the round space above the gates when they were shut, and a red curtain was drawn slowly behind the sun. The choir sang. The air was warm with body heat and candle flames. People kept bowing again and again, all the while making the sign of the cross. One old woman, in black, ragged, felt slippers, her black, torn stocking sagging, a black rag wrapped about her head and neck, almost bent her head to the floor each time she bowed, and she never stopped rapidly crossing herself. In the midst of these people, Joe stood motionless.

Frowning, Zoya leaned toward Joe and whispered, "You do not pray?"

"I would like to leave."

Zoya nodded.

As they left, he saw, at the back of the congregation, the KGB man, who was standing with his fur hat in his hand and his head bowed low.

The dark sky seemed to have sunk to the earth, with street-lights and house lights buried in it. Zoya didn't talk to Joe. Outside the hotel were only a few prostitutes. They appeared to approach Zoya but she stopped them by turning away. She said to Joe, smiling slightly, "Our KGB man stayed in church and gave up following us."

He tilted his head to one side.

They stood in the light that came through the glass revolving doors of the hotel, beside which the commissionaire took a stance as if to let no one in without a hotel pass.

Zoya said, "I am sorry I took you to church. I didn't know that, perhaps, you are against prayers and religion."

"I thought religious services were forbidden in the Soviet Union."

"That, like everything, is changing. Are you disappointed?"

A laughing couple came out of the hotel, and Joe moved out of the way to let them pass.

Zoya remained where she had been, then, as Joe didn't move, she went to him and said, "Am I doing what American woman would never do to man, asking if I can see you again?"

Joe, sure he had seen her before in just this place at just this time, said, "Tonight, come to have dinner with me in the hotel."

She smiled a smile that was slow but that finally revealed one stainless steel tooth at the back.

The woman from whom he had to get the key to his room was not at her desk. Joe walked up and down the corridor until she appeared. He presented her with his hotel pass and she gave him the key, neither one looking at the other.

From the freezing outside, he found his room so hot he sweated. The window didn't open. Naked, he lay on the bed in the dimness behind the dusty green velvet curtains.

Maybe, he thought, he shouldn't see Zoya again.

In the suffocating heat, he felt sweat drip down his armpits and his groin as he fell asleep. But he was drawn back from sleep by shouting and the stomp of feet, and he recognized the voices of the American children running along the outside corridors, now near, now far. He heard, in the distance, something break, like glass crashing, and the children shout, "Let's get out of here."

He tried to sleep for an hour, thinking of seeing Zoya again, because he was frightened to be left alone.

He fell asleep and was woken by the telephone ringing. Dazed, he answered, and a man spoke in Russian. Joe hung up.

He looked about the room, where the woman from the church, weeping into her handkerchief and her face wet with tears, appeared to be standing in a corner.

T W O

Zoya never came that evening, and Joe, alone, could not make himself go out.

He stayed in his room and, as with the urgency to save himself, tried to imagine himself somewhere that would be different from anywhere he had ever been. But he could only imagine himself back in that brown clapboard house in the New England woods; could only imagine himself, on a hot summer afternoon, wandering through all the rooms of the house.

When he made himself at least go down to the hotel restaurant, a big woman shouted at him, *"Zagrit,"* which he knew meant closed, but beyond the woman standing stolid at the entrance he saw that the restaurant was packed with people, waiters rushing among the tables with raised, silvery trays. He couldn't argue. He returned to his room and lay on his bed.

He was in Russia, but he imagined himself outside the house

in the New England woods, wandering about and seeing the house through the trees.

He suddenly heard himself say, Imagine.

Imagine? he asked himself.

Go ahead, he said to himself, try to imagine some place where you never before imagined yourself or anyone to be.

Lying on the bed, he closed his eyes.

He imagined himself walking toward the back door of the house in the woods to go back in and wander from room to room, but he stopped at the bulkhead by the door. He imagined himself studying the bulkhead with a sense that it led down, not just to the cellar, but to a place he had never before been to. And he imagined opening one of the slanting doors to the bulkhead.

On his bed in a hotel in Russia, his eyes closed tightly, he urged himself to open one of the bulkhead doors and look down the cement steps, lit up halfway down by sunlight.

He smelled damp earth and mold. He felt the cement cold and rough against his bare soles as he descended the steps. He saw pale light beam in through a small, oblong window onto the dirt floor. Another window was blocked with cement cinderblocks. In a corner was a stone sink and, standing in a puddle, an old clothes-washing machine with a wringer. A rusted tin tub hung on a cinderblock wall. Deflated inner automobile tiretubes were piled by a roughly made brick wall that had a doorway in it to another part of the cellar.

Joe stood before that open doorway and with a slight shiver said, "God save us."

He entered the boiler room, where the furnace was encased thickly in dusty asbestos and the tank for the oil was covered with cobwebs. The floor was dry earth. There was no window.

Beyond the furnace was a wooden door, made of warped,

unpainted planks and with a rope handle, which Joe had never before seen. Opening it, he peered into, then entered, a small room with old, uneven brick walls. The floor was thick with gray dust, and in the gray dust lay half-buried broken wine casks, and there were footprints to a part of the wall that appeared recently bricked in. On a stone nearby was a trowel. Hanging out of a hole in the newly bricked-in wall was an arm, reduced to skin and bone; it rose a little and the fingers of the hand reached out and remained reaching out for a long moment before the arm dropped.

No, Joe thought, not this.

At the back of the room was an old, heavy, paneled door with a shiny black knob that gave onto a long narrow corridor, and Joe went down the corridor to another wide, heavy, paneled door with a shiny black knob, and in the door was a small, barred window through which Joe looked.

He saw beyond the bars into a room whose walls were lined with torn and stained mattresses. Lying on a dirty mattress in the middle of the cell was a naked woman, her body tied so tightly with nylon stockings her back was arched. Her mouth was forced open by a stick jammed between the roof of her mouth and her bleeding tongue. A naked man, his back and shoulders and chest matted with black and gray hair, was standing over her. Her head and body were shuddering, her eyes wide open on what the man was about to do to her.

Joe shut his eyes and thought, And not this, something beyond this, something you haven't seen yet, something so different the world hasn't seen it yet.

He opened his eyes. The woman was no longer there. Joe went into the cell, and as he did, he shut the door behind him, and it locked. In the cell was silence, then, faintly, the distant sound of water sloshing.

What he'd seen in this cell he'd only imagined, and he hated what he imagined. But, looking about, he saw the amputated breasts in the dirt on the floor, and splattered against the mattresses along the walls were bits of organs and bloody fat and flesh.

No, no, Joe thought, he had to be able to imagine more than this. He had to be able to imagine a place that had never been imagined by anyone in all the history of the world.

But the door to the next room was as he expected it to be: a metal door, partly rusted and flaking where the paint remained. And he already knew what was going to be behind it if he opened it, knew that he'd find a low room with a metal grating on the floor, under which water sloshed. He knew this would be the room the operations took place in, on a steel operating table with an acetylene lamp hissing above it. And at the center of a circle of naked men and women, all having contorted sex with one another, a woman in high heels with a scalpel was operating on a young man strapped to the operating table. He was gagged with adhesive tape. The woman cut off his cock and showed it to him, cut off his balls and showed them to him, cut off his ears, nose, cheeks, and showed them to him, and then she cut out his eyes. Even while Joe stood behind the closed ship's door, he knew what was happening behind it, so there was no reason to open the door to see if what was happening would be different.

There had to be something we hadn't ever seen, he thought, had to be something no one had ever imagined, so different from what anyone in the world had ever imagined it had never in fact been seen, something that could occur only by God making it occur.

Heavy and rigid on its rusted hinges, the door resisted his opening it, and he threw his body against it to shove it wide open, but it opened slowly—with, yes, a groan. The room was empty except for the hanging lamp, extinguished.

Joe crossed the room and opened a sliding steel door and saw a long, cobbled alley, and at the end of the alley the dim light of a city street. Outside on the black cobbles he thought, But this, too, everyone, everywhere, has imagined. And when he saw, in the streetlight at the end of the alley, a truck with people packed together in the back, he thought, And this, too; this, too. The alley remained quiet, and Joe, hunched, ran down the side of it trying the doors of the small stone houses he passed, but they were all locked. And when he got to the street, he ran to a cement hut at a bus stop to hide.

There he found a girl in a nightdress pressed into a corner, shivering, and he thought, No, not here, somewhere else, somewhere I could not have expected.

As he reached out to put his arms around her, she drew back with wide and terrified eyes, and he knew before she spoke what she would say, stuttering: that they must escape, that they must find somewhere to hide before dawn. He ran after her as she ran out and down the street, but as he had known would happen, the truck turned a corner so they were now running toward it.

Everything that followed was as he expected it, everything— He and the girl were shoved into the back of a truck packed with terrified men, women, children. The truck took them out of the city into flat country. The truck, at dawn, stopped before a wooden gate of a ranch on a wide, grassy plain with roaming buffalo and woods and mountains in the far distance. The high fence around the ranch was coiled with barbed wire.

God help me to think of something else, he thought, as, hit in the head by a rifle butt, he was herded into the camp, where he was separated from the girl. Even if it is worse, even if it is so much worse than this, God help me to think of something I would never, ever have been able to expect, what world history would not let anyone expect. That's what I want, that's what I want helplessly to give in to—not this, which is everything I knew would happen, but something that has never, ever before happened to anyone.

But it was just as he expected. He saw a bare, muddy lot surrounded by barbed wire, and more barbed wire uncoiled, in huge spirals, across the lot, and in the midst of the coils were groups of naked men and women, their heads shaved, reduced to bone and skin, the groups being commanded to race from place to place by guards in uniforms hitting them with clubs and rifle butts, breaking jaws, ribs, skulls, so some of the prisoners, falling as they clutched their bleeding faces, were trampled on by the feet of the racing groups and the—oh, yes—boots of the guards.

As Joe, shoving people aside, searched for the girl in the skeletal mass, thinking, I know this, I know it, he felt his arm wrenched by a guard and he was hurled into a group racing from place to place. Just able to balance himself, he, startled, found himself racing among them. He shouted out, All the world knows this, but he realized that, if the guards were shouting orders and the prisoners were screaming, no voices were heard, and there was silence. He saw the girl ahead of him among the racers and he ran faster to catch up with her, but she ran even faster to win the race. Trampling over prostrate bodies, his skin caught on and torn by the barbs of the wire, pushed and shoved aside by the people he was racing with, trying to reach the girl, he shouted, but without sound: I know all this. And the rest happened as he'd known it would happen: he reached the girl, but, on impulse, he raced past her, and as he did, he turned only once to see that she, fallen behind, was taken apart and made to stand at the edge of a muddy pit.

And in the next race he fell behind and was commanded to stand among those who had fallen behind, the girl among them, all at the edge of the muddy pit. And when there were enough couples, men with women, men with men, women with women, they were forced to have sex. Down the line, the girl was in the arms of an old man. Joe put his arms about a trembling girl whose nipples on her small, gray breasts were tight and cold and whose rib cage, backbone, hipbones stuck out, but they were not able to have sex, as much as they both tried. And as Joe knew would happen, black rain fell.

What he wanted was something he didn't yet know. Everything, everything depended on his being able to imagine something he didn't yet know, but what only God could let him know, depended on the world being able to imagine what the world didn't yet know, but what only God could let the world know.

All he was able to see was this—that he and the girl he had tried to have sex with, that the girl and the old man she had tried to have sex with, that the other couples who hadn't been able to have sex no matter how they had tried, were pushed together and their throats slit. Their bodies fell, twisted on one another. Joe, dying among the arms and legs of people he didn't know, thought, But no, no, there's something else for us.

He saw his naked body thrown into a ditch among the other dead bodies, the bodies below sliding against one another with the impact of his body falling on them. He saw a bulldozer heaping earth over the bodies. He saw the marks of the bulldozer treads in the mud.

Was he the only one, ever, to imagine that something of him rose from the mud crisscrossed by the bulldozer tracks and walked away, walked over a vast, blasted landscape with poles with wires strung from one to the other and a loudspeaker on top of each pole, walked beyond the poles into a country where snow was falling and was blown into drifts against trees, walked into a forest until he came, in the snow, to a brown clapboard house with a fieldstone chimney tangled in a bare honeysuckle vine, before which he stood, his hands over his face?

Joe sat up when he heard a knock on the door. He didn't answer. The room was dark. Rigid, he waited for someone to come into his room, but no one did.

THREE

GOD HELP ME IN THIS.

FOUR

Joe was sitting in the compartment of the Red Arrow express train to Moscow, now in the station in Leningrad. He sat on the low berth, made up with sheets, a thick gray blanket, and a small pillow, and he looked out the window of the compartment onto the dimly lit platform of the station. Snow was falling on the people outside carrying bags to their assigned berths. The snow fell slowly out of the darkness of the sky.

He was waiting for Zoya, who would sleep in the other berth, also made up. As he sat still, he had one of those moments of feeling he was being pulled, pulled as if by ropes tied around him and yanking at him, and he went rigid trying to draw himself back from that pull.

He looked from the berth to the door to the compartment when it slid open on Zoya, her face flushed from the cold, and with a sudden sense of relief, he jumped up to help her put the suitcase on the rack above her berth.

She said, "When I saw you just now, you had such expression of grieving on your face. What is wrong?"

He laughed. "Nothing is wrong."

Standing near her in the narrow space between the berths, he helped her take off her coat, then her hat, and her long hair, tucked up, fell loosely and heavily. Her smooth face became pale.

He said, "I have brought a bottle of champagne and some sausage and bread."

Clapping her hands, she said, "I see you want to have good time."

"As good a time as we can have with bad, sweet champagne, hard sausages, and dry bread."

"And I see you can tease."

"I like to try."

"But we have no glasses. I shall get glasses from attendant."

The attendant, an old woman in a uniform with the insignia of the train on the breast pocket of her jacket and most of her teeth missing, brought them two tea glasses in metal holders. Zoya said something in Russian to her, and she, with a limp, left and came back with another glass. Joe opened the bottle and poured the foaming champagne into the three glasses, and they all touched the rims of the glasses to one another and raised them, and Joe said to the old attendant, *"Tovarich,"* before he drank. The old woman laughed.

Zoya said to Joe, "She thinks you are joking with her, calling her comrade."

"Me, joking with her?"

The champagne foamed in the toothless spaces of the attendant's gums when she drank, then, laughing still, she again left.

"Everyone's going to think I'm teasing," Joe said.

"Aren't you?"

Joe smiled.

Zoya said, "I am sorry I was not able to be with you so much in Petersburg. You shall see, we shall be a lot together in Moscow. Moscow is my city."

"I did interesting things in Leningrad."

"What?"

"I saw in the Museum of Religion and Atheism in the former Kazan Cathedral how evil religion has been to the people all over the world."

"I know you are joking. You could not have been serious when you went there."

Smiling more, Joe said, "Oh, but I was. I do think religion is evil in making us believe in what isn't there."

"Joe, Joe, do not say that."

"Don't tell me that you, a Soviet, believe in another world when you already live in the best world?"

Zoya, clapping her hands once and holding them together, said, "I do."

"I wonder if you're joking."

She seemed not to know if she should laugh or not, and when she did, she said, separating her hands in a wide gesture, "I wonder if we are both joking."

Joe asked, "So what did you do while you were in Leningrad?"

"I wasted my time. I did nothing I was supposed to do, nothing."

"What were you supposed to do?"

"You really are little boy, asking questions you shouldn't."

"All right, then—why didn't you do what you were supposed to do?"

"Because I didn't want to do it."

"Why didn't you want to do it?"

"Again, your questions." Zoya took the bottle from Joe, filled their glasses, drank from hers, and said, "I didn't want to do what I was supposed to do because I decided I didn't want to do it."

Her eyes were more thickly outlined with black liner, her lashes blacker with mascara, than before, as if going to Moscow required this added makeup, and he noted, too, a slightly tawny rouge was brushed on her broad cheeks.

She said, "I decided, after I met you, I did not want to do it."

Zoya looked at him, looked into his eyes, and he felt an unbearable sense of being pulled down, which made him lie back on his berth.

She said, "When I ask you what is wrong, you tell me nothing."

"Nothing is wrong."

"Every time you say that, I worry more about you."

"Why do you think there is something wrong with me?"

"Because I feel that you are denying there is."

Joe shook his head.

"We will have fun in Moscow," Zoya said. "We will tease one another."

"I'd like that."

"Now we will get ready to sleep."

"I'll go out into the corridor while you get ready."

Zoya pulled her black angora sweater, which she wore all the time as if she had nothing else to wear, over her head, which left her long hair in tangles. She was wearing a bra.

"I have been told," she said, "in America men and women

are never put into same sleeping compartment. In our Soviet Union, we are much more advanced about equality of sexes."

"I've always thought the United States had something to learn from the Soviet Union."

Joe went out into the corridor while Zoya in the compartment undressed. Though he looked out the window of the moving train, he could see nothing but darkness. Male passengers, wearing pajamas and large, unlaced shoes, passed him to use the toilet. Joe drew back from the window to let them pass, and he saw their reflections in the window and beyond their reflections that vast darkness. The men used pomade on their hair, combed flat. Joe kept trying to see a light outside illuminating a pylon, a factory chimney, a house, but there were no lights at all.

Zoya slid the compartment door just wide enough to show her face, and she asked, "Shall I stand outside while you get ready?"

"No, I don't mind."

"I'll get into my berth."

He waited outside a moment longer, then went into the compartment and slid the door shut after him. The light inside was brownish yellow. Zoya, her knees up, was lying under a thick brown blanket, the white sheet folded over it, her head raised on two pillows in white cases. Her hair was pulled back and braided at her nape, and the braid hung over a shoulder. She was wearing a white night shift.

She smiled. "I won't look."

"I don't mind," he said again, and he undressed, facing away from her, and put on his pajamas. He got under the narrow, rough sheet and thick blanket. The wagon swayed, and his body and head rocked a little from side to side.

"Shall I switch off light?" Zoya asked.

"If you'd like."

She didn't switch it off. She was looking at him, smiling. Then she turned off the yellow light by a switch over her head and the compartment filled with a dark blue light. Joe couldn't see her in it.

The compartment was hot, and Joe, reaching down, tried to unfold the heavy blanket doubled on him, but only managed to twist it, along with the sheet, so he was half-uncovered, and he wasn't able to straighten the blanket or sheet. Leaning out, he raised the blind to try to find a way to open the window, but it was shut with mingled rust and paint around its frame. He lowered the blind.

Now, used to the blue light, he was able to see Zoya in her berth. She was lying on her stomach, her face turned away, the braid dragged out on her pillow. He listened to hear her breathe, but couldn't hear.

He kept being rolled toward the edge of his berth by the swaying motion of the train, and he saw, over that edge, into such dark openness, he quickly, quickly, pulled himself back. Each time, it seemed to him, he looked down into a great dark space in which images occurred—

He saw in the darkness a clump of birch trees and near them a red, wooden lawn chair and through the trees a brown clapboard house.

He, as if physically, drew himself back from the darkness in which the image occurred.

The train stopped, and with it a juddering motion in the very air of the compartment stopped. In the silent stillness, he turned to look across at Zoya and saw that she had turned toward him.

She asked quietly, "You can't sleep?"

This so shocked him, his arms flew out.

She laughed and, rising a little, put her hand over her mouth to stop the laughter. "I'm sorry, I frightened you."

"No, no."

"But I did."

"It's all right if you did."

She laughed again. "Why will you not tell me what is wrong?"

Joe didn't answer, but swallowed, then opened and closed his lips a number of times with the slight, liquid sound of his tongue pulling away from the roof of his mouth.

There was the clang of iron bars striking iron wheels, and the train, with a strain and a sudden lurch, began to move.

Joe lay back.

He was woken by the wagon attendant, and it seemed to him he was in the middle of the long night. The attendant gave him a glass of hot tea and a paper-wrapped sugar cube, which Joe sat up to take. Zoya was already sitting up, drinking her tea through a sugar cube held between her teeth. The attendant raised the blind of the compartment window. It was still totally dark out. Zoya didn't say anything, but Joe knew she was looking at him. He held the glass of tea to his lips and took long pauses after each sip.

"Joe?"

He tried to turn a smile to Zoya.

"You will tell me what is wrong."

Trying to smile more, he said, "But there is nothing wrong."

"Why do you deny?"

"What do you think I deny?"

"Your grief."

This shocked Joe as he had never before been shocked by anything anyone else had ever told him, and shocked, he raised his arms toward her, then dropped them. She stared intently at him but he turned his face away, and he kept his eyes turned away when she got up and dressed. He kept his eyes on the rim of his glass.

"We'll be there in five minutes." She had undone her braid and was combing out her long hair. "You'd better get up."

He threw back the disordered berth covers, and Zoya, still combing her hair, left the compartment and slid the door closed behind her.

When she came back inside, Joe, dressed, was sitting on the edge of his berth.

"Don't you want to use the toilet?"

"Yes." His voice sounded like a pubescent boy's that suddenly went out of pitch.

"You'd better go then."

In the corridor, he passed male passengers in pajamas. The toilet was a stinking, brown-and-yellow hole, and it roared with the dark below. He peed, then for a moment held his penis in the palm of his hand. Outside, a man in pajamas was waiting to use the toilet. His pomaded hair stuck up at the top.

Zoya was standing outside the compartment by her valise. Her fur hat and scarf were on, and she held her suede coat over her arm. The train was slowing down.

"You'd better get your bag down," she said to Joe.

He did, and as she was putting on her coat, she said, "You'd better put your coat on."

He did.

"And your hat."

As he was putting on his hat, the train stopped and unbalanced him.

He followed Zoya out of the train onto the platform, where

the low lights shone just above the crowd of passengers walking toward the exit.

Out in the street, Zoya told Joe to wait at the curb while she looked for a taxi. The streetlights seemed to shine hardly higher than the fur hats of the people walking along the crowded pavement, and above the lights, above a layer of grainy, gray, diffused light, was all dark sky.

Zoya hadn't found a taxi, she said when she came back to Joe, but a private car whose driver said he'd take them for a dollar.

There was no snow, and the streets, with little traffic, appeared wide. Along the pavements on either side, pedestrians, in long overcoats and fur hats and boots, walked in masses, while above the low layer of electric light was that high, high, dark sky.

"Where are they going?" Joe asked.

Zoya answered, "They are, like good Soviets, going to work."

FIVE

JOE, CARRYING HIS AND ZOYA'S CASES FROM THE CAR, followed her to the back of a cement block of apartments into a long, narrow, rough, weed-grown yard, and through a battered door into an entrance hall. The hall was painted pale blue, with rows of darker blue mailboxes on which numbers were painted crudely in white strokes, and near the boxes was a partly rusted metal box, tilted and held to the wall by a rusted bracket across it. Above the box, Zoya pressed a combination of buttons and turned to the inner door into the foyer of the apartment building, expecting it to open, but it was still locked. She had to press the buttons again and again until the door, which seemed about to fall off its hinges and could have been pushed open, opened.

"Soon," she said, "nothing, but nothing will work, nothing."

The walls of the elevator that took them up were scratched

with graffiti, and the car rattled, stopped for a moment between floors, then, with a little jolt, continued up.

Zoya sighed.

Joe took in all the details, as if it were in the smallest details that Russia would be revealed to him: on the landing, the door, padded with brown vinyl and studded with brass tacks, which Zoya opened with a key; the small entrance hall with walls covered with, it appeared, layers and layers of thick, gray wallpaper, mottled with stains and, however thick, showing the cracks beneath; the floor covered with irregular bits of brown felt, glued down and worn; and just inside, tacked to a wall, a tourist poster of a view of the Rocky Mountains of America. Joe followed Zoya directly ahead into the one room of the apartment, papered in blue paper with a pattern of many, many small white and yellow medallions, with gilded light brackets, here and there at angles on the walls, holding up bare bulbs on imitation dripping-candlesticks, a few dirty crystal prisms hanging below. The floor was creaky parquet, the spaces among the boards wide and impacted with dirt, and in the middle of the floor was a cheap Turkish rug. There were two cubelike chairs, the foam-rubber stuffing showing through tears, and a sofa. On the sofa lay an old teddy bear with one leg, which looked as though it had been soaked in water, and a pile of blankets and sheets and pillows.

Looking about, Zoya again sighed. "I used to think of this as luxury place before I brought you here."

"You probably have a very elevated idea of the places in America where I've lived."

"I have no idea at all of places in America where you have lived in."

The room was hot, and the heat smelled of dust, grease, and faintly of shit.

"We cannot control heat," Zoya said. "Comes from government heating center, maybe kilometers away, through pipes underground. You will see steam rising out of ground in empty lot or at street corner, and you will know that a pipe bringing steam heat has broken underground. You will see that all over Moscow. Now is too hot, but, suddenly, there may be no heat, and room will be freezing cold."

"Whose place is this?" Joe asked, taking off his fur hat and gloves and coat and throwing them on an armchair.

Zoya removed only her hat, which she waved as if it didn't matter whose place it was. "I suppose, really, I should register your presence here with police, but I think police, now, would not know how to register foreigner in private apartment, if that is permitted, which it most likely is not. I think for you to stay in private apartment you would need to have permission from Soviet embassy from when you were in America, so it would be on your visa. So, because they will say they can do nothing to give you permission to stay, we will not go to police."

"I'll be staying here illegally?"

"Does that worry you?"

"It worries me, yes, not to be doing everything strictly legal in the Soviet Union."

"Would that worry you in United States?"

"No."

"But here, yes."

"I want to do what's expected of me here."

"You want to be thought of as good boy, like Young Pioneer always doing what is right."

Joe smiled.

"Don't worry. No one here does what is expected, or right. You will find out that Moscow is totally corrupt city, where what is legal is what you can get away with, and you can get away with everything, especially if you have American dollars."

"I changed five hundred dollars into rubles when I first arrived."

"You were crazy. No one will accept rubles. You still have dollars?"

"I have."

Joe felt that Zoya was about to ask him how many, but she restrained herself. She said, pointing to the sofa, "You will sleep here. You did not sleep on train and are tired, I see, so sleep now. Russians sleep on sofa, not because we want to, but because our apartments are too small to have bedroom. Did you have bedroom to yourself in your house?"

"I did, yes."

"Was it big house?"

"It was a big, brown, clapboard house with a cellar and two floors and an attic with a steep roof and gables, and it was in a forest."

"A deep forest?"

"Well, a woods."

Zoya appeared to be trying to imagine it, but a thought broke through and abruptly she returned, now in a hurry, to instructing Joe about the apartment. She showed him the bathroom and the kitchen.

"Do not," she said, "answer telephone if it rings. Or, rather, in case I might be telephoning, pick up receiver, but do not speak until you hear me, and if anyone else speaks, you say nothing and hang up receiver. If telephone rings again immediately after, do not answer."

Zoya didn't go. In the main room again, they stood before a wide window with a view of a cement apartment house exactly like the one they were in.

Zoya asked, "And in America, did you have job?"

"I was a student."

"What did you study?"

"History."

"And you gave up?"

Joe said, "It's begun to snow in Moscow."

For a while, standing side by side, they watched the snow fall in slow flakes.

"In where you lived in America," Zoya asked, "did it snow like it does here?"

"Yes."

"So much that everything was covered deeply in snow?"

"Very deeply."

The snow began to collect on the broken pieces of furniture out on the little balcony.

Then, as if, again, she remembered she was in a hurry, Zoya said, "I must go."

But she remained standing still beside Joe.

"The snow is falling more heavily," Joe said.

"You do not want to talk about America." With apparent great reluctance Zoya turned away from Joe and left him standing at the window, and putting on her hat and picking up her case, she went out of the apartment.

It was only when Joe, his case open on an armchair, was sorting through what he had packed, wondering if he should take anything out and if so put where, that he realized he was locked in the apartment. Zoya hadn't said when she would be back. He walked around the room, trying to calm himself down. He thought he might panic.

The telephone rang and he went stark still. It rang and rang, a large, black, old-fashioned telephone. Joe gently raised the receiver but said nothing. A loud voice asked, "Zoya?" Joe held

49

the receiver to his face without moving. He heard again, "Zoya? Zoya?" and he hung up. Immediately after, the telephone rang again, but he didn't answer.

He looked in his case for his toiletry bag, and as he was turning over his underwear, he uncovered a money belt. He took it out and unzipped it and ran his thumb over the thickish edge of a book of traveler's checks, all the money, except for a few hundred dollars in bills, he had left from his part-time job while he'd been studying. He extracted a ten-dollar bill from the money belt and held it in his hands. What did it mean, he thought, this American ten-dollar bill in Soviet Russia? He put it back and took from his toiletry bag his toothbrush and toothpaste, his razor and shaving foam, and he went to the small, windowless bathroom that smelled very much of shit.

Zoya was right, he was tired because he hadn't slept on the train, and he should, now that he had brushed his teeth and shaved, sleep. But his being alone in the apartment kept him wandering around it.

Don't panic, he told himself; don't panic.

A wide piece of furniture against one wall consisted of cabinets at the bottom and shelves behind sliding glass doors at the top. All the books were in Russian, and propped against them were black-and-white photographs, curling about the edges, of slightly out-of-focus people in an apple orchard, the branches of the trees hanging low with fruit, and all the people laughing.

Joe put the photographs back on the shelf. He had taught himself to read the Cyrillic letters, but couldn't make out any book that was written by Marx or Lenin or any Communist, though some of the books had their spines missing. And nothing, nothing at all in the apartment, referred to the history of the Soviet Union, and apart from the books, all that referred to Russia was, on a desk, a wooden bowl painted in a black-and-red, Slavonic pattern that was filled with pencil stubs, common pins, and pinecones.

He was making up the sofa with a bottom sheet and a blanket inserted into a cover that was like a large white envelope when he heard the door to the apartment open, and he called, "Zoya?"

A thrill of fear went through him at the sight of a large man in a large brown fur hat and a long, brown overcoat, unbuttoned and swinging open on his bulging stomach, his face red.

"Who are you?" the big man asked in American English, as if this were the only language he spoke and presumed everyone in the world understood—not because they understood English, but because they must understand *him*. He didn't wait for an answer. "Were you the one who answered the telephone?"

"I—"

Again, the big man didn't wait for an answer. "Where is Zoya? She was supposed to meet me. I waited five minutes for her in the snow."

Joe wondered if the man was joking and laughed a little. "That's long enough to die in the snow." The man did smile a little, but not enough to reassure Joe that he'd been joking. "She was here, but said she had to go."

"Who are you? Were you the person who answered the telephone when I called?"

"I—"

"Never mind who you are. Don't go on making up that sofa, which is so uncomfortable you wouldn't be able to sleep on it in any case. You can't stay here."

Wondering again if the man was joking, Joe asked, "You're going to send me out to die in the snow?"

The man grunted in a way that might have been a little laugh. "Is that meant to be funny?"

"I hoped so."

The man now did unmistakably laugh, and Joe relaxed. If Joe could make a person laugh, even a little, he felt that everything would be all right, that the person would like him.

But the man shook a hand loosely at Joe's open suitcase and said, "You'll have to close that and go. I told you you can't stay here."

He offered no apology and no reason for Joe not being able to stay, and he would not, Joe knew, wait to hear from Joe why he was there. His large face, made smooth by fat, was redder than when he had come in, with sweat running from under his fur hat and down his cheeks. His blue eyes were small and round and bloodshot. He turned away and left the apartment.

Joe sat on the sofa and looked about the room. He hadn't noticed a pair of worn felt boots beyond the bookshelves, and a broken chair in a corner, and propped behind the chair a big, cracked, empty picture frame that had once been gilded. He sat for a long while.

With some effort, he got up and began to arrange his clothes in his suitcase so he could close it. There came over him once again not only the fear of being alone, but of being alone in the Soviet Union, where he knew there were rules and regulations that were strict and that he must obey. But he didn't really know what these rules and regulations were. It seemed to him that by going out alone into Moscow he was going out into a world in which anyone could stop him and tell him that what he was doing was wrong, even carrying a suitcase in the street. He closed his suitcase and put on his overcoat and fur hat, and he went to stand by the window to look out at the snow falling more heavily, now covering the broken pieces of furniture on the balcony.

He was standing there when he heard Zoya call him and he turned to her.

Alarmed, she asked, "Where are you going?"

"A man came and told me I had to go, so I'm going."

Zoya closed her eyes for a moment and in a low voice said, "So Gerald came here." She opened her eyes and said, "I wanted you *not* to meet Gerald."

"If that was Gerald, I met him."

"He never comes to this apartment unless we have business. Why, now, did he come looking for me?"

"Maybe because when he telephoned earlier and I answered and said nothing when he asked for you, he came to check this place out. You were late meeting him."

"But I was five minutes late."

"He seemed to think that was long enough to die."

The snow on her boots melting, Zoya walked around the room, trying, it seemed, to make up her mind what she should do now. "It does not matter if he met you. He will forget he did. He will not mind your staying here, because he will forget that he told you to go. Gerald says things like that, without even thinking of what he is saying. He doesn't mean what he says. He doesn't mean what he says because he doesn't think of what he says. He says he minds waiting, but then, another time, he says he doesn't mind waiting, for however long. You never know what Gerald will say. He says, only, what first occurs to him without thinking. And then he forgets what he said."

"He seemed to mean what he said."

"Please believe me. He did not mean it. If he came back now, you would see that he had forgotten to tell you to go.

Without even asking how you are, because it never seems to matter to Gerald who anyone is, he would tell you to sit down and would offer you vodka because that is what first occurs to him. And then he would tell you to stay in apartment."

"Supposing something else, not so welcoming, first occurred to him?"

"With me here, only to tell you to sit down and to offer you vodka would occur to him. Gerald is always different when he is with me."

She pulled off her hat and threw it on a chair, then took off her coat and threw that on the chair, then untied her boots and threw them from her. "I did not want you to meet him, but now you have."

"Why didn't you want me to meet him?"

"Because you are good, like boy is good. Gerald is not good, is too much of man to be so good as you are." Swinging out a hand in a wide gesture, Zoya said, "Gerald is in our Soviet Union for the truth of what our Soviet Union is now, and Gerald is here to make money out of collapse of our Soviet Union. I mean, *the* collapse. You see, talking with you, I am beginning to remember to use articles."

"What's his business?"

Zoya put her hands to her face and held them there in silence, then she dropped her hands and stood. "I must go and find him and tell him I did not do in Petersburg what he expected me to do, and that I have put you up in this apartment. He will not mind either that I did not do what I was supposed to do in Petersburg or that you will stay here."

"You won't tell me his business?"

"It is business we have together."

"What is that?"

Zoya approached Joe and pulled a little at both wings of his collar as if to bring him closer to look more deeply at him. He saw she was very tired. "You would not fit into our business."

"You and Gerald are partners?"

"We have, in a very loose sense, what is called joint venture. In our country, *joint venture* has become Russian expression now. I was supposed to come back from Petersburg with some-one who would fit into our joint venture, but I did not. In Petersburg, I thought, I won't do it, it is stupid, all stupid. So I came back with you instead."

"And Gerald won't mind?"

"Gerald, I tell you, doesn't mind anything. He doesn't care about anything, not even our joint venture."

"I'd like to know what that is."

"I help find people who want to leave Soviet Union for West, and Gerald helps them to leave."

"And why this apartment?"

"Here, people who are to leave in a few days stay while waiting. It is for people in transit."

"In a way, as I am."

"Let us go out and buy at least some bread and kefir for you to have in kitchen, in *the* kitchen. Do you know what kefir is, a yogurt drink? Kefir is still one good thing you can find in our Soviet Union. We will buy some if the lines are not too long in the shop."

"I thought you said you had to see Gerald. I think you should see Gerald. Gerald might get angry if you don't see him as soon as possible."

"Yes, yes, Gerald." Zoya bit her lower lip. "Gerald."

She went to the telephone, dialed, but over and over the call didn't go through, and angrily she jabbed at the buttons at the top until the telephone emitted a faint jingling ring, and when she dialed again, the call went through.

SIX

Zoya paced about the room. She clasped her hands together and squeezed them until the knuckles were white, then she unclasped her hands and let them drop, two red fists, to her sides.

She said to Joe, "If you knew Gerald, you would see how funny he can be. As funny as you. I think Gerald will like you. If you say amusing things, he will like you. Try, please, to say amusing things. Gerald likes, always, to be amused. And he gets bored so easily, especially if someone is serious. He cannot bear anyone to be serious, cannot, especially, bear anyone to be serious about himself."

"I'll do my best not to be serious about myself."

"You make me laugh. Make Gerald laugh," she pleaded, "please."

"I'll be as much the joker as I can be."

"He will talk a lot. I have to tell you, he will talk a lot. If he is drunk, he will talk more than if he is not drunk, but that is all right, because at least when he is drunk—" She sighed.

"At least when he's drunk, he's even funnier than when he isn't?"

"Yes, funnier."

Pacing about the room, one of her big toes sticking out of a hole in her stocking, Zoya suddenly hit her head with her fists. "What I know about Gerald is that, underneath all his talking, talking, talking, underneath his wanting always to be amused and his easy boredom with anyone who is too serious, underneath his being funny, he is . . ."

"What?"

Zoya wailed slightly when she said, "He is not good man, but he is good to me."

"Good to you?"

Joe sat back in the armchair, heavy with the realization of what Zoya meant by "He is good to me." That could have only one meaning, and thinking, Of course, of course, Joe closed his eyes and leaned his head against the grease-stained chair back.

"Joe?"

Opening his eyes a little, he asked, "What?"

"Try to like Gerald."

"I'll try."

"It will be difficult. It is difficult for me sometimes. But, I tell you, he is good man to me."

"*A* good man," Joe said, "rather than a good boy."

Pretending to doze, he closed his eyes again. It came to him that he did not know where he was, or why he was where he was, or whom he was with or why he was with her, because all the explanations of why, which up to this minute he hadn't questioned but which he'd felt he could answer if he had questioned them, seemed now to have been taken away from him—taken away by her saying, simply, that Gerald was good to her. He would never, ever be able to be as good to her, he was sure, never. He, a boy, was not capable.

He heard Zoya say, "Yes, you should sleep before Gerald comes to be ready for him," and he let his head roll to the side.

Zoya had no reason to worry. He wouldn't take himself seriously when he was with Gerald, not because he didn't want to bore Gerald, whom he did not want to see, but because Joe was incapable, ever, of taking himself seriously when with anyone else. That he could only do when he was alone, and when he was alone and being serious, he felt he was so alone and so serious he could never be with anyone else. Now, he suddenly felt as alone and as serious as a boy who had not reached puberty when everyone he knew of his age had, and that was because Gerald could be good to Zoya and he could not.

Joe turned his head from one side to the other, and the smell of dust from the chair back rose about his face.

With a jolt of his body, he heard Zoya say, "Gerald," and he realized that he had fallen asleep.

He opened his eyes to the sight of a big man removing a huge brown overcoat and, doing so, listing unsteadily in different directions. As he let the coat slip from his arms, Zoya, rushing to him, grabbed it and put it on the chair before the desk at the other end of the room. There was a large bottle of vodka, a loaf of bread wrapped in newspaper, and a carton of kefir on the low table before the sofa.

The man said in a loud voice, "You'll be pleased to know I'm totally drunk," and with his long, thick fingers he wiped spittle dribbling from the corner of his large mouth.

Though drawing back in revulsion, Joe thought, I'll make

him like me, not for Zoya, not for myself, but just to do it, I'll make him laugh.

Joe stood and held out his hand to the man.

Gerald, frowning, looked at Joe's hand and after a moment asked, "What's that for?"

"For you to bite."

Gerald did laugh. "That's nice of you." But he turned away from Joe's hand without touching it and asked Zoya, "Who is this person?"

She didn't answer. "Shall I get glasses for vodka?"

"Good idea. Yes, get some glasses for the vodka. You always have such good ideas, Zoya, such as glasses for the vodka, instead of our drinking it out of our cupped hands." Gerald fell backward onto the sofa that Joe had half made up with sheets and blanket, fell so heavily the piece of furniture shook.

Zoya picked up the bread and kefir and went into the kitchen. Gerald, leaning back, looked up at Joe, who remained standing and waiting for the man to speak, but all the man said was, "Open the bottle of vodka." Laughing as though opening the bottle were a joke, Joe did what he was told, so when Zoya returned with three small, delicate glasses etched with white flowers, Gerald said to Joe, "Now fill them up," and Joe, laughing more, did this.

As Joe, feeling now that he couldn't help himself from laughing, handed a glass, the vodka trembling about the rim, to Gerald, the man said, "I like to see someone having a good time."

"I'm having a very good time," Joe said.

"Go on having a good time and you'll go a long way with me, boy, a long, long way—all the way to wherever I'm going, which is a long, long way away." He raised the rim of the small glass to his lips.

Zoya stopped him from drinking by exclaiming, "But we must have toast."

Gerald lowered his drink a little. "These damned Russian toasts. I never know what to toast. But if a toast is required, let there be one. Let no one say that I don't respect the conventions of a culture I live in but am a foreigner to. In England, in the best circles, no one would ever propose a toast, never. But that was in England, and now I am in Russia, though perhaps in not quite the best circles, and in Russia there must always be a toast." Gerald raised his glass toward Joe. "Whoever you are, you propose it."

"Please, you do it," Zoya said, anxiously looking from Gerald to Joe, "propose toast."

Joe tried to think of something that would get Gerald joking with him. That was what Zoya wanted him to do, but again, he wouldn't do it for Zoya, but because he himself wanted to joke with this big, repulsive man, who wore an old tweed jacket and a polo-necked shirt with its collar so stretched it exposed all his fat neck and whose enormous penis bulged in the tight creases at the crotch of his unpressed trousers.

Once, maybe not too many years before, Gerald had obviously been a handsome man, which would have been evident if the sag under his chin had been pulled in to show more of his strong jaw, if his jowls had been tightened against his cheekbones, if the dark circles around his small, blue, bloodshot eyes were lightened. Waiting for Joe to propose a toast, he pulled at his polo neck and stretched it even more.

Joe said, with a laugh that surprised him for being so out of his control he might already have been drunk, "I propose that we drink to sex."

"Here, here," Gerald said, "to sex," and he drank his vodka down in one gulp.

Joe, unable to control his laughter, couldn't drink, and he knew his inability to control his laughter came from the sudden, hysterical delight in being with this grotesque man, who was Zoya's lover.

Gerald said to him, "Drink up, drink up. I'm polite enough that I wouldn't have another until you've drunk up yours."

But Joe's hand was shaking with his laughter, which, as hysterical as it was, was silent.

Worried, Zoya said to him, "Drink up, Joe."

Joe spilled some of the vodka as he drank down the glass.

He then said to Zoya, "But you haven't drunk."

Frowning with worry, she poured the vodka into her raised, open mouth and swallowed it all at once so her long, slender neck convulsed.

Gerald said, looking at his empty glass, "Good idea these glasses. I'd have hated to drink the vodka out of my hands, it'd have poured through my fingers." He held out the glass toward Joe, expecting Joe to refill it, and Joe, now trembling with suppressed laughter, filled it, then filled Zoya's glass, then his own.

Vodka spilling from the full glass held in his right hand, Gerald wiped the saliva dribbled down his chin with his left hand by stretching the collar of his polo neck. Then, his extended left hand flat, he gestured to Joe and to Zoya to sit, and as if he assumed they wouldn't unless he gave them permission first, he said, "Sit, sit." They sat. And he was generous in his giving them permission to drink when he commanded, "Drink, drink." Joe and Zoya waited for Gerald to gulp down his before they gulped down their vodkas. Again holding out his glass to Joe, Gerald said, "Now fill us up again."

Serving this man gave Joe a twisted pleasure, a pleasure that, as twisted as he knew it had to be, tickled his fancy, and bowing as he tilted the bottle, he laughed as though he had in fact been tickled. He tipped the bottle back, then said, "Wait, there's room for another drop," and tilted the bottle back to pour out, carefully, one drop, which made the liquor swell a little above the rim.

Gerald said, "It'll spill."

Joe said, "I'll bet I can add still another drop without it spilling."

"Try, and if it spills, I'll make you lick it up from the floor."

Delicately, Joe poured out another drop, and the liquor swelled precariously about the rim, but was held.

Gerald asked Zoya, "Who is this guy?"

Zoya, who understood and didn't understand Joe's bantering, but trying, herself, to be like Joe, said, "Oh, Joe's a strange person who shared my compartment on the train from Petersburg."

Joe said to Gerald, "I'm very, very strange."

Gerald liked this. He was amused by Joe, and Joe knew it, and Zoya, too, knew it. Gerald laughed, or maybe he laughed—some deep, inner impulse, activated, tried to raise and animate his body, but it was only able to rise enough to make his large shoulders go up and down like a shrug and make his lower lip stick out with a grunt that sounded something like "Ha." He drank his vodka as it was spilling down over his glass.

Then he said to Joe, "Go on about how strange you are."

Zoya said, shaking her hair out, "Joe is too shy to tell you."

"Shy with me?"

"You *are* daunting presence."

"*A* daunting presence," Joe said.

"So I'm told, so I'm told, though I find it difficult to understand why. I think of myself as anything but daunting, someone even thrown out of a miserable little café on the Arbat for knocking over a table. Me, thrown out of a miserable little café on the Arbat, where all they said they had to serve was tea and slices of dry white bread when I asked for a coffee with cream and a piece of chocolate cake."

"It was an accident," Zoya said to reassure him, no doubt having had to reassure him over and over again about this and other events in which he knocked over tables. "You know it was an accident."

"They thought I was a monster."

"No, no, no. They didn't understand."

"No doubt I am a monster."

"No, no. You are not monster, but daunting presence, and you make people shy."

"They weren't shy in the café."

"But they didn't throw you out. They stood back, daunted. You left."

"That's right. I left." Gerald held out his empty glass to Joe again and commanded a refill, and while Joe refilled the glass, Gerald asked him, "Who are you?"

"I'm Joe."

"You're the very, very strange guy."

"Yes."

"Who's also shy."

"Yes."

"Drink up your vodka, Joe, and have another," Gerald said.

"With your permission," Joe said, smiling.

"You have my permission, boy."

Zoya said to Gerald, "You see how polite Joe is."

Gerald swigged down his glass of vodka and said, "Being as you're so polite, Joe, before you drink your vodka, pour me another." Joe had to rise from his chair once more and with the bottle lean toward Gerald, who made no effort to extend his arm, his empty glass hardly held out. He grunted when Joe, smiling with delight, filled the glass so it brimmed, then he said, "Pour in another drop, and if it spills over the edge, I throw the glass into your face."

Joe's constant tremor of laughter made it difficult for him to hold the bottle steady. He had to concentrate. The large, round drop fell heavily into the vodka in Gerald's glass and swelled it around the delicate rim, but the liquor didn't drip over.

Zoya laughed a high, nervous laugh.

Gerald didn't compliment Joe on his dexterity at filling a glass higher than the rim, as though what had counted for Gerald was not Joe's doing it but his failing. Gerald held out the glass, the liquor trembling, and said, "That was a significant toast, your toasting sex."

"I'm glad you liked it."

"Drink, drink."

"You first," Joe said.

Gerald swigged his vodka, then Joe. Zoya held an empty glass, which she turned round and round in her hands, and when Joe lifted the bottle to her, she drew her glass against her bosom and shook her head.

"No doubt about it," Gerald said, "the collapsing Soviet Union is just the place, now, to toast a whole new world of sex, because for seventy years there has been no sex in the Soviet Union—I can even say it in Russian: '*V S.S.S.R. sexa nyet*'—and the people are as ready for it as suppressed peasants ready, brandishing raised scythes and sickles, to claim their rights. There will be sex in the collapsing Soviet Union as has been unknown anywhere else in the world. And I am here to help things along, aren't I, Zoya?"

Zoya only smiled a thin, tight smile.

Gerald said, "I am rather proud of the fact that I am descended from Carolina carpetbaggers who knew a good thing when they saw it in the collapse of the American South. There are possibilities here in the Soviet Union, oh, yes, there are possibilities. Aren't there, Zoya? And I am helping Russians realize the possibilities, aren't I?"

Keeping her thin, tight smile, Zoya nodded.

"Aren't I helping you?" Gerald asked her, and in the look Gerald gave Zoya, his eyes bulging and as if filmed so that they appeared blank and shiny, Joe saw his possessiveness of her, and in her look back, her eyes sharp with her fear, Joe saw her dependence on his possessiveness of her. It more than thrilled Joe to know that Zoya and this grotesque man were lovers, that his penis, bulging in the folds of his crotch, was, when erect and sticking out from under his fat belly, presented to Zoya as her duty. Joe wanted to let Gerald know he was aware that he and Zoya had sex, and he wanted Gerald to know he was pleased, he was even overcome with joy that they had sex. When, now, he laughed, he knew his laughter was crazy, but he thought, Let it go, let it go, let it be crazy.

"You think it's funny that I'm helping Zoya?" Gerald asked Joe.

"I think it's great."

"What does your friend here know about my helping you?" Gerald asked Zoya.

Zoya laughed apprehensively. "I think he has drunk too much and only imagines what."

Joe had drunk too much, and drunk as he was, Joe *desired* Gerald to have Zoya, he *desired* Gerald to have Zoya to do whatever he wanted with her. Joe would, himself, give Zoya to Gerald for Gerald to do with as he wanted even if Zoya hated what Gerald did, even if Zoya were helpless in her suffering of what Gerald did, because Gerald *should* do whatever he wanted.

"Let him imagine whatever he wants," Gerald said, and he sat more deeply among the bedclothes on the sofa. "I have great respect for Russia, would never want to offend anyone in doing the wrong thing, such as bringing someone an even number of flowers, which is bad luck, or shaking hands over a threshold, which is bad luck, or doing any of the many, many things that bring bad luck. I am very sensitive to the ways of this country, aren't I, Zoya?"

"You are very sensitive."

"But that doesn't mean that Russia can't profit from my presence, isn't that so, Zoya?"

"We Russians have a lot to learn from joint ventures with Westerners. We Russians have everything to learn."

"You will learn, you will learn, Zoya."

Gerald held out his glass again to Joe for a refill, and refilling it, Joe realized that as much as Zoya believed that Gerald was a good man trying to help her, in fact Gerald had no intention of helping her, had no intention of helping anyone. And maybe Joe was pleased to realize this, pleased to realize he was serving a man he knew was evil.

"Fill my glass," Gerald again commanded Joe, who rose again to do what the big man commanded.

Zoya pressed her empty glass between her round breasts.

Gerald said, "If I had been taken seriously, as I should have been, I could have been an American senator, like my father. And I don't doubt that, had I become senator, I would have made it to president of the United States of America. But no one took me seriously." Gerald drank down his vodka in one gulp. "And no doubt everyone was right not to take me seriously, because the fact is I am not serious, I never do what I say I will do, and I am totally incompetent. And I have never helped and will never help anyone." He said to Joe, "You

wouldn't believe me, would you, if I told you my life is utterly
and totally a failure, utterly and totally without promise. And
I accept this. I accept it."

Gerald should have the power to do anything he wanted to
the whole world and anyone in it, Joe thought, anything at all.

"Do you believe me?" Gerald asked Joe.

"I believe everything you say."

"Well, if I'm not going to help anyone, least of all myself,
I'm going to have some fun. You know that, really, don't you,
Zoya? You know that I never do what I say I will do, you know
that I'm totally incompetent, and that I won't ever even help
you, but I will have fun with you?"

"Please," Zoya said.

Joe wanted to hear about the vanity of the very desire to
help. He wanted to hear of the vanity and defeat of anyone
anywhere who had ever even had the idea of being good and
helping anyone.

And all the while, he felt rising in him his grief, rising to
break out in a high, wailing laugh.

Gerald said, "If I had been, as I should have been, president
of the United States of America, I would have helped people,
I would have helped my fellow countrymen by saving our re-
public."

"How?" Joe asked.

"I can't remember, and don't want to remember, because
there's no point in remembering. America has failed, and nothing now can be done to save her. Not even I could save her.
America has failed, failed, failed—" He made a dramatic gesture, then, his hand held like an airplane making a nosedive,
he suddenly froze with self-consciousness; but he held the pose
against his self-consciousness, held it for the drama of it for a
long while, long enough for the drama of it to show up as an

intention and to impress, and knowing he had impressed, he smiled and dropped his arm. He said nonchalantly, "Now let's have another round of vodka. You, too, Zoya, you, too."

Zoya was made to hold out her glass and Joe filled them all.

Gerald said, "America has destroyed itself and as the most powerful country in the world will destroy the world. It's the end of America and it's the end of the world." Gerald puckered his fat lips and seemed to be thinking about what more he could destroy, and as he thought, he spread out his lips into a wide smile of pleasure and knowingness. "It's the end of everything."

Joe wanted to hear about the end of everything, wanted to hear about the vanity and failure of believing in anything at all, the vanity and failure that reached out in every direction as widely and as deeply as space itself, and more than in any other way freed him from his own vanities, made his vanities as nothing in the ego-less infinity of failure far beyond his ego.

Still smiling, Gerald said, "Shall I tell you the essential truth? It is the great American capitalist truth, and it is the truth that will make Communist Russia fail. The essential American truth is this—that, no matter how committed a person appears to be to his country, to the world, no matter how much he worries about the very fate of the earth, he is committed really to himself only, he is worried really only about his own fate. Everyone knows that the selfishness of each and every individual, whose rights to selfishness are guaranteed by our American Constitution, is the destruction of our country, the world, the very earth. Our Constitution upholds the right to destroy the world, and the world *will* be destroyed, utterly destroyed, and those who remain among the ruins will be committed, each and every last individual, to himself only, will worry about his survival only, and will, by constitutional right, cut down the last remaining tree that might, if it were saved, produce enough seeds to replant the forests of the world, kill the last couple of birds that might, if left, reproduce a flock of birds to replenish the fowl of the world. Society, culminating in the inalienable American rights to life, liberty, and the pursuit of happiness, has evolved in an essentially wrong way for the world to survive. It is all wrong, but it is the basic American truth of the world that you are you and I am I, and I am glad that your being poor doesn't mean that I must be poor, your being ill doesn't mean that I must be ill, your suffering doesn't mean I have to suffer, your being black or a Jew or a queer doesn't mean I have to be black or a Jew or a queer, your dying doesn't mean I have to die. I am very glad that in the USA we live individually and we die individually. As wrong as it is, as destructive of the very earth we all live on as it is, I am glad that the only person I have to care about is myself. And that makes me American."

"Please," Zoya said, turning her empty glass, "please."

"A Soviet is, of course, different. A Soviet doesn't think about himself, but only about others. Isn't that so, Zoya?"

"Please."

"In the USSR, your happiness is my happiness, your health is my health, and, especially, your money is my money. Only the Soviet belief in selflessness can make the world worth living in, can save the world. In the Soviet Union, everyone thinks only of the happiness of everyone else, and everyone else's first concern is to help everyone else. Soviets are always rushing to help one another, aren't they, Zoya? What a vision, what a wonderful vision, the USSR started out with to save the world. Almost a religious vision. In fact, it *is* a religious vision, unlike the crass antireligious vision of the USA, because everyone knows the best religious visions are based on selflessness. The world might have a chance of surviving if the vision of the USSR wins out over the vision of the USA, so all the world should thank God for Communism."

"Gerald, I ask you, please."

"But the unfortunate truth is that that wonderful, religious vision is a lie. We can't live lies, no, no."

"Please, Gerald, please," Zoya implored yet again.

"And you know what will happen in the USSR? The great lie will give way to the truth, the truth that has for almost a century has been denied to the people of the USSR. And they will rise up and revenge themselves against all those years during which they were denied the truth, and they will do so by acting on the absolute conviction that any life other than your own is worthless. They will act on the essential truth of our individual selfishness with such ruthlessness, with such crass justification of the most brutal forms of capitalism, with such cruel indifference to the lives of other people, America will be shocked by them, shocked. Russia will become *more* true than America, and finally come into her destiny of taking over the world by destroying the world in a way that will make America seem like the world's protector."

"No," Zoya said to Joe, "no, Gerald is not right. Don't believe him, Joe, don't. Believe me when I tell you Russia is and will be different from what Gerald says. Russia loves and cares for her children. That is why we call Russia our mother."

"You are all orphans," Gerald said, and frowned and delicately touched an eyebrow with a long, fat finger, then sighed a little. "How boring all this is. But what isn't boring?"

In his massiveness, Gerald appeared to be above even impressing anyone, because he didn't care, he didn't care what he thought and said about anyone and what anyone thought and said about him.

Loosely holding out his empty glass yet again, Gerald said to Joe, "You're not being very attentive to me. You should fill my glass as soon as you see it's empty."

"I'm sorry." Joe reached for the bottle, but lifting it said, "It's as empty as your glass."

"The bottle empty?" Gerald asked in a tone of amazement. "Who drank it all? Now what will we do? We can't sit here without vodka."

"I will go out and buy bottle," Zoya said.

"I'm not going to drink any of your gut-rot vodka sold at a corner kiosk for rubles," Gerald said. "You'll have to go to a hard-currency shop to buy the real stuff."

"I will go to hard-currency shop."

To demean her, Gerald said to her, "You know that as a Soviet you are not allowed to have hard currency. Supposing you're arrested in the hard-currency shop just when you're paying for the bottle in—?" He hefted his large body to take his wallet from the back pocket of his trousers and, opening it, took from it bills from different countries—American dollars, British pounds, Belgian francs, German marks—and he held out the wad toward her, but when she made a tentative gesture to reach for for it, he drew it back. "You haven't answered me. What will you do if you're arrested with hard currency in your possession?"

Zoya's face tensed, but tensed, she tried to laugh. "If I am arrested, what will *you* do?"

"Find another Russian girl who'd like to go into a joint venture with me."

"You think that would be easy?"

"You know how easy it would be."

Joe said to Zoya, "I'll go out with you and buy another bottle of vodka from a hard-currency shop."

With an impatient and commanding gesture, Gerald said to him, "You stay."

"Stay," Zoya said to Joe. "Stay with Gerald."

When Gerald said absolutely, "Stay with me," Joe felt a sense of pleasure, and maybe, too, reassurance. But he got up and said, "I don't think Zoya should go out on her own."

She grabbed his hand and looked at him with an expression of pleading him to stay. "You have drunk too much to go out."

Swaying, he realized that he had drunk so much he could hardly remain standing.

Gerald held out the wad of bills to Joe and said, "Let go of her hand and give this to her."

Joe quickly pulled his hand from Zoya's and with it took the bills from Gerald and gave them to Zoya, who bowed her head on her long neck when she took them.

"I'll help you on with your coat," Joe said.

"Do not bother."

"I will."

As, swaying badly, he helped her on with her coat, he saw that Gerald was watching them. Joe not only held the suede coat with the torn lining out for her, he walked with her, however much he swayed, to the door to the apartment and opened it for her. Putting on her hat as she left, she whispered, "Go back to Gerald. He likes you. I knew he would like you."

"I think I should come out with you."

"No, please," Zoya said, stepping out onto the landing, "go back to him for my sake."

"For your sake?"

"For my sake." Turning away from Joe, she looked down at her bare hands and exclaimed, "Agh, I have forgotten my gloves, and I cannot go back into apartment for them, is bad luck to go back for something you forget. Please bring me my gloves."

Joe was aware of Gerald studying him as he looked for Zoya's gloves, found them on the desk, and brought them to her.

"Are you so superstitious?" he asked.

"I have every reason to be superstitious."

He watched her put on her gloves, which had holes at the tips of the fingers.

She whispered to him, "Do not believe what Gerald says about Russia. He is kind of American who has always wanted our Soviet Union to fail, because he knows that our Soviet Union is morally superior, because he knows that our Soviet Union is conscience for United States, and he wants to destroy that conscience by making USSR worse than USA." She put a gloved hand on Joe's hand. "I know you are different kind of American." She tried to smile. "Please go on amusing him."

Joe withdrew his hand from Zoya's and she turned and rang for the elevator and he turned back into the room. From time to time having to get his balance by touching a piece of furniture, he walked around. He didn't want to sit before Gerald again.

But Gerald said, "Sit down."

Joe sat before him.

"What'd you say your name is?"

"Joe."

"Tell me, Joe, what do you like?"

"What do you mean, what do I like?"

"What do you *like* is what I mean."

The way the man said this, as if he were flatly sober, made Joe feel that he was being asked what most other people would not only not admit liking but would not have known anyone else in the world also liked.

"What do I *like?*"

"That's the question I asked."

Joe's head lolled from side to side, then he let it hang, his chin on his chest.

He heard the man say, "Maybe you should study me carefully to learn how to avoid, at all costs, becoming like me." Gerald laughed and again pulled at the collar of his polo-necked jersey, stretching it more.

His head hanging, Joe laughed, then he raised his head to look at Gerald.

"I was brought up in a world that in itself made me capable of anything," Gerald said. "My father was a senator, and I lived in Washington. And as I grew and became known, I was invited to all the parties. I was invited because the hostesses knew that I would be offended if I was not invited and would be cruel about them to others, and hostesses are terrified of people they know will be offended, deeply offended, if they are not invited and will then say cruel things about them. I was dumb like you, but I learned, with effort, to say cruel things about people, especially hostesses. They also knew that I could revenge myself against them by what I knew, and what they knew I would say, about them. But I said what I knew about them anyway. I always did, and they were aware I did. Still they invited me."

Joe tried to keep his head up.

"My advice to a young man such as yourself is—however dumb you start out being, put all your creativity into learning cruel wit. Learn to keep everyone laughing, especially about the people everyone else envies, the rich and the famous and the powerful. Make your wit outrageous and cruel. Everyone will love you. Well, perhaps I should qualify—not love you, but forgive you for being cruel, forgive you, too, for the monstrous egoism of knowing so much about the rich and the famous and the powerful—if you can tell them stories about the rich and the famous and the powerful that will make them laugh. They will forgive you up to a point, and I, I must say, passed the point. And that was fine with me, because I wanted to go on anyway."

Joe's head began to fall sideways, and he righted it.

Gerald said, "Was I born that way, or did something happen to me? I don't know, or don't remember if it ever happened. In fact, I don't think anything did happen. Stories about horrors in a person's past that are meant to justify what a person is now are always excuses, and I loathe excuses. I have never claimed that something horrible happened to me when I was a boy to excuse me for what I am now. No, no. I had a perfectly sound and protected childhood, even a privileged childhood, as people who were eager to get into my father's good books thought that being nice to me—taking me up in private planes to New York to see Broadway shows—would get them in. I don't try to excuse myself for what I am, never, because I have no excuses. I have never suffered." He pressed his lips together. "I had everything. I had good looks, money enough, intelligence, social connections, and I learned cruel wit. And if I must blame anyone for my failure, it can only be myself. But I don't blame myself."

Joe put a hand to his head to try to steady it.

"You haven't told me what you like, Joe."

Joe dropped his hand and let his head loll.

"Do you like Zoya, Joe?"

"I like Zoya, sure I like Zoya."

"What would you like to do with Zoya, Joe?"

"What do you mean, what would I like to do with Zoya?"

"You know what I mean? Would you like to fuck Zoya? Would you like to do more than fuck Zoya in the cunt, Joe? Would you like to do anything at all you wouldn't dare yourself to imagine to Zoya when you're fucking her?"

Joe hung his head low.

"Do you want me to tell you what you could do to Zoya when you're fucking her that maybe you haven't fantasized about, not even in your craziest fantasies? Look at me," Gerald commanded.

Joe raised his face and Gerald stared at it for a long while. Then Joe closed his eyes.

The room was winter dark when Zoya came in and lit the bulbs without shades in the wall brackets. Her hat and coat were white with snow. She put the full bottle of vodka on the table next to the empty one, then took off and shook her hat and coat. She also took off her wet boots. Gerald and Joe didn't move. "Have you been so silent all the while I have been away?" Not waiting for an answer, she went into the kitchen for the bread and kefir. She said to Joe when she came back, "You must eat. Gerald, I know, will not. But you must." Joe ate a piece of bread she tore from the loaf and drank the yogurt drink from the carton.

Gerald said, "Is no one going to open the bottle of vodka and pour out a drink for me?"

Zoya did this hurriedly, and this time she did not stop Gerald from drinking by asking for a toast.

"Pour out a glass for your friend," Gerald said.

"I think that he has drunk enough."

"Pour it, I tell you. And pour yourself a glass."

Zoya did as she was told, and both she and Joe raised their glasses and drank as they were told.

The heat in the room was so thick with dust that Joe felt he could hardly breathe. He must, he thought, open the glass door to the little balcony at the other end of the room, but as he tried to stand, he fell back into his armchair. Again and again he tried to stand, and each time he fell back. Gerald and Zoya did nothing but watch him. Slowly, holding on to the arm and then the back of his chair, he stood, then, after getting his balance, he walked the length of the room to the glass door and opened it onto the outside cold, which he breathed in. He saw nothing but snow falling in the darkness. Leaving the door open, he turned back into the room, and he walked up and down the room, each time stopping at the open glass door to breathe in the cold.

He turned away from the glass door and approached Gerald, slouched on the other side of the low table, which, with the bottles and glasses, was puddled with spilled vodka. Joe fell to his knees and rocked back and forth.

The low table before him was kicked to the side, so the bottles and glasses crashed to the floor, and Gerald stood before him shouting, "Get up, get up."

But Joe couldn't get up. He leaned so far over in his keening his forehead touched the floor.

Zoya was behind him, her hands under his arms, trying to lift him, but he nearly pulled her over onto him with his rocking back and forth.

She cried, "I knew there was something terribly wrong, I knew, I knew."

Gerald, above him, shouted, "I told you to get on your feet," and this so startled Joe, he became still. Again, Gerald shouted, from deep in his throat, "Get on your feet," and Joe tried to, but slipped and fell back. Zoya put her arms about him to help him, but Gerald shouted at her, "Let him do it alone," and she jumped back. His hands pressed against the floor, Joe struggled to raise one leg and then the other, and for a while he remained crouching, too weak to stand on his own. Zoya again put her arms about his shoulders to help him up, and once he was up, Gerald shouted at her, "Let him go," and she let him go. Joe, shaking, had to keep pulling himself back from falling, and all the while Gerald, standing so close to Joe he felt Gerald's spittle on his face, barked, "Who do you think you are, kneeling before me?" Joe, shaking so he couldn't control his shoulders and arms, tried to stand at attention. Gerald shouted, "You mean nothing to me."

Zoya, moving nervously around them, called out, "My God, my God. The police will come. My God."

Terrified, she went near enough to Gerald to reach out her arm from too far a distance for him to strike her, and she touched his shoulder. The big man immediately fell backward onto the sofa, his eyes open.

Zoya put her arms about Joe and, whispering, said, "Sit, please sit," and he weakly let her guide him to his armchair.

She, too, sat. After a while, she laughed a little and said, "It is as if we were sitting in silence before we go off on a long trip."

Joe slumped forward.

SEVEN

The boy was woken from his dream by the sounds of ice breaking on the river. There were whines and groans, then, suddenly, violent screams that came nearer and nearer, louder and louder, booming from one bank of the river to the other.

In the morning, the boy met his father going to see the prince and said to him, "The ice on the river is breaking up."

"And you want to go see it."

The boy nodded.

He went with his father to the prince, who was sitting beside the little round table with the half-drunk glass of goat's milk on it. This morning the newspapers, which the prince had always folded and placed on the table after reading them, were thrown about him on the floor. He sat with an elbow on the arm of his chair and his hand on his forehead, and his two Samoyeds, sitting up with their paws together, looked at him but stayed back. The prince was in a padded dressing gown, worn at the elbows and neck.

When the prince raised his head from his hand, he saw his bailiff and his bailiff's son, and he smiled at the boy. But he said to the boy's father, "The world news is very bad."

"I know only the news of the estate."

"Shouldn't you know more about the world?"

"Would that make our lives on the estate better?"

"You're right, you're right." The prince sighed and, looking at the boy, said, "And perhaps it would be better for your son never to know anything about the world."

The boy, next to his father, listened to him and the prince talk about the estate, the running of which the prince left to his bailiff, and then his father put his hand on his son's shoulder and said to the prince, "We are going to see the ice breaking on the river."

"I know how much we Russians love to see flowing water after a freezing winter," the prince said.

"Will you come with us?" the boy asked the prince.

The prince passed a hand across his forehead and said to the boy, "You come with your father to dinner and tell me about it."

As the bailiff and his son were leaving, the prince stood and picked up the newspapers and folded them.

Peasants were gathered along the bank of the river, and the boy pressed in among them to watch cracks appear in the ice, fissures widen, and pieces of ice detach themselves and, sinking and rising, flow down the channels, bumping along the jagged sides, stopping where other pieces were jammed together in a passage too narrow for them to get through, so more and more pieces congested, tipping against one another at odd angles, until, as if giving way to them, the passage widened and they flowed through on black, leaping waves. Branches, wooden crates and casks, sometimes broken pieces of furniture, appeared among the ice floes. Some of the peasants of the estate had long boat hooks, and with these they tried to hook the crates, casks, furniture, but the hooks were not long enough and swung out without reaching.

Farther down the river, a peasant was pushing a horse onto the ice. The horse, an old one, resisted being pushed onto the ice, but it was too weak and gave way to the peasant, who was pressing against the horse's rump with his back. The horse stumbled forward, its front hooves struck the ice, slid, and it fell forward onto its knees, hitting its head, then it fell onto its side and rolled over onto its back. The peasant was shouting curses at it. With difficulty, its hooves slipping, the horse managed to stand again, its legs splayed, and turned and stared at the peasant, who kept shouting curses, now making gestures with his arms as if to push the horse away. But the horse, slipping from side to side as it stepped, walked back onto the bank. The peasant simply watched as the horse came up to him and pressed its nose against his chest, pushing him back.

His hands out, the peasant thrust all his weight against the horse's head, and the horse jolted backward and again stumbled and fell onto the ice, which cracked under it. Before it could stand, the peasant picked up a long boat hook and started to swing at it from the bank, and when it did finally stand, the peasant struck its legs. As it fell, the ice opened under it, and it sank headfirst, but it emerged, its front hooves trying to get purchase on the broken slabs of ice that tipped under it, and neighing with a high sound that the boy had never heard a horse or any other living creature make, its neck muscles straining to keep its head above water. The current took it, along with a tree and a wooden crate and a broken table, and it sank under the floes.

Meanwhile, another peasant picked up the boat hook the peasant had used and with it reached out into the river of ice floes and debris to hook the prow of a small boat, which he pulled toward the bank. In the midst of the turbid, flowing water, the boat was filled with clear, still water.

The prince was waiting in the dining room for the bailiff and his son to return from the river. The boy, unable to eat, sat in silence, and when the prince, after a spoonful of fish soup, said to him, "Now tell me what you saw," the boy stood and ran out of the room.

After the bailiff described the incident by the river, the prince pushed back his chair and went out to find the boy. He found him in the hall, standing against a wall, staring out.

The prince said, "Listen."

Silent, they listened to the sounds of the river.

The prince said, "I know the world is terrible. But a different world, a world so different we can't now imagine it, will replace this world, you'll see. It will not be for me to see, but that doesn't matter. It will be for you to see. You must believe that."

EIGHT

UNDRESSED DOWN TO HIS UNDERPANTS, JOE WOKE on the sofa in a confusion of sheets with the blanket out of its cover. The room was freezing cold, so cold he saw his breath steam about him when he raised his head to look about. He was shivering, but when he tried to sink more deeply among the bedclothes for warmth, he uncovered a bare shoulder, a leg, a thigh. He could not remember who had undressed him and put him to bed, but whoever had, had then left him. The glass door to the balcony at the other end of the room was still open, and the central heating was off. Snow blew into the room on the freezing wind. Joe had no idea, from the dull gray light, what time of day it was; as there was only daylight, it seemed, between late morning and early afternoon, the time could have been any hour in between. Again, he tried to cover himself over with the bedclothes, but the freezing air blew in at all angles.

He ran quickly to the bathroom, where the smell of shit made him gag, but there was a bathtub, which used the same long, swinging tap as for the washbasin next to it, and he plugged the drain with a rag and turned on what should have been hot water. But the water was cold, and it got colder and colder as it filled the small tub. He felt not only freezing, but dirty, and he plunged his hands up to the wrists into the cold, clear water. Quickly, he pulled off his underpants and stepped into the tub and splashed the cold water about his body, soaped it, and splashed with water again. The cold seemed to burn his skin like flames. He jumped out and tried to dry himself with a small towel, but his body remained damp, and shivering more than ever, he ran to the sofa where his clothes had been thrown at the foot and he dressed. He put on his overcoat.

It was difficult to close the glass door because a small drift of snow had piled against it, but he forced it closed and for a while looked out at the snow falling so thickly he couldn't see the apartment buildings across the backyard.

He thought of being in a great forest in the falling snow, a forest so great it would seem to cover the entire world, a vast taiga.

He took his money belt from his suitcase and buckled it about his waist, under his overcoat, then buttoned his overcoat. As he had not unpacked, it did not take him long to flatten out his clothes in his suitcase and shut it. Then he put on his gloves and fur hat. He was aware that if he left the apartment, he wouldn't be able to get back in because he didn't know the combination number, and standing out on the landing with his case, he held the door to the apartment open for a long while before, slowly, he shut it, knowing that when he shut it, the door locked and he did not have the key. The elevator down got stuck between floors, and he had to press the down button to start it again. He was shivering a little, and when he opened the door out into the snow, he felt the cold through his over-coat and shivered more. The door shut behind him.

A great cloud of steam rose with a hiss at the back of the snow-covered yard, the steam mingling with the snow, which must have meant one of the steam pipes Zoya had told him about had broken underground.

Joe left the yard. A strange sense came to him as he walked the snow-covered streets and passed people that he had been in these streets and passed these people before. The feeling he had was the same feeling of having known Zoya before. In fact, he couldn't have walked along these streets before, as he couldn't have known Zoya before. But the sense made him stop under a scaffolding of wooden planks attached to the facade of a building with a notice, PEMOHT, nailed to it, and he thought, I know this place. He even knew the word meant "renovation." Looking at the people pass him, their heads bowed against the snow, he thought, I know these people. Yet, he couldn't make himself ask any one of them where the near-est metro station was. As familiar as they appeared to him, he felt that he didn't have the right to talk with them and they didn't have the right to talk with him.

Among the dark, hunched people appeared a young woman, walking straight and smiling into the falling snow and wearing a fancy kerchief tied about her head and a bright pink cloth overcoat, and Joe wondered if she was a prostitute.

He walked on, his case heavy, so from time to time he stopped and put the case down. Whenever he stopped, differ-ent men, but all it seemed in brown overcoats, came quickly to him and said they would change his hard currency for rubles at a better rate than the official rate, but Joe shook his head. He passed apartment buildings with children's playgrounds among them, the slides deep in snow. He stopped on a corner.

An official-looking man, wearing an astrakhan hat and a camel-hair coat with wide lapels, came toward him eating sunflower seeds, cracking the shells with his teeth and throwing the shells away to eat the seed. He looked at Joe as he advanced, and Joe, holding out a hand, said, *"Pazhalsta,"* but the man, with a military bearing, turned his face away quickly and walked past.

Joe saw, coming from the direction in which the military-looking man went, the woman in the pink overcoat. Maybe she had seen him and had decided to backtrack to talk with him. As she approached, smiling a wide smile, he saw she was hardly more than a girl, her face red from the cold and redder high on her cheeks with brushed-on rouge. She looked at him as she passed, but he said nothing, not until she was a little past him and he called softly, *"Pazhalsta,"* and she turned, smiling as before, to him.

"Metro?" he asked.

She couldn't speak English, but signaled him with an unraveling pink knitted glove to follow her, and she brought him to the entrance of a metro, Oktjabrskoye Pole, where, smiling the same smile she had had all the while, she left him. Maybe she wasn't a prostitute.

At a ticket window, he changed a ruble note into kopeck coins and, as he saw other people do, inserted a coin into a slot by a turnstile and pressed his way through. Joe could make out the names of the stations, and also what changes he should make to get to the train station he had arrived at from Leningrad.

In the crowded metro, the passengers surrounded him in total silence and stared out into space.

He came out of the metro to the station, which in the falling snow looked like a delicate, abandoned palace. But inside it was dark, with yellowish lights here and there that did not illuminate but were reflected in the wet cement floor, and the station was packed with people in dark overcoats. There were long lines at all the ticket windows, if they were all ticket windows. Joe did not know where he should go to be deep in the Russian forests, but he thought that anywhere far enough outside Moscow would be far enough. And if he didn't know the name of any town in the forest where he might buy a train ticket to, he would buy a ticket to Leningrad and get off when he saw from the window a town that was deep in forest. He joined a line, not knowing if he would be able to buy a ticket to Leningrad from the window it led to, but it was the smallest line, of about thirty-five people, and he thought that, surely, it would be possible to buy a ticket to such a big city as Leningrad at any window. The line of people moved one step, and Joe took his step and put his case on the wet and dirty cement floor. A man came and stood behind him, and Joe felt a little confident that if the man behind him had joined now, it must mean the man assumed he would get a ticket. Joe kept urging himself to turn to the man and ask, "Leningrad?" and point to the ticket window, where there was a pale yellow light, but he couldn't get himself to do it. Though cold, he was sweating.

Again, the line moved a step forward and Joe hefted his case to step with the line. Maybe he should have left his case behind, as, an encumbrance, he would have no use for anything in it. He should have left it behind because, somewhere along the way, he would have to get rid of it, along with everything that identified him—not only his passport and American money, but his American clothes. He would have to go into that great snowbound forest naked.

He saw the forest, saw the high, dark trees, saw the snow falling among the trees, and he saw himself, naked, walking toward a deep drift.

For a long time, the line he was in was static. He became impatient and often looked at his watch, which no one else in the line did. Then the person at the head of the line left and Joe thought the whole line would take a step forward, but the woman behind the ticket widow reached up and pulled down a blind. An hour passed and the line did not move. The blind went up on the ticket window and the same woman looked out at the first person in the line. Joe thought he felt too low to become angry, but he did become angry, and after the second hour, during which he took only two steps ahead, his anger rose into panic. He couldn't stand still, not only checking his watch every moment but looking over the heads of the people before him and taking tiny steps forward as if to urge the line ahead with his chest, then stepping back. Every half hour or so the woman ticket seller drew a blind over the window and left it down for, it seemed, a half hour. Joe didn't think he had it in him to be violent, especially not now, but his hands folded into fists and his arms began to twitch when three hours passed. He thought he would easily kill the woman behind the ticket window if he could get to her. Whenever she drew down the blind, he told himself to leave, just leave, but his anger, his hatred, his desire to kill, would have ended only in defeat if he left, and he would not give her the satisfaction of knowing she had defeated him, which was what she intended. Before him and behind him, the other people in the line stared out into space. After four hours, Joe was tenth in the line, close enough now to see the woman seeming to fill out forms. Joe shifted his weight from one leg to the other, over and over. His only comfort was to see himself walking into that forest, where he would lie in the snow and fall asleep. When he was fifth in line, the woman behind the ticket window, frowning, reached up and drew the blind down over the window. The people in the line stood for a little while longer, then, staring out as they had been staring for hours, they walked away, and Joe, defeated and knowing he had been for a long time sure that he would be defeated, picked up his case and walked away with the dispersing people.

With his case, he stood outside the station in the snowy darkness. His sinuses were blocked and his nose running from his cold, and the only tissue he had was a wet, gummy ball.

The feeling came to him to simply lie down there where he was.

He walked slowly into Moscow, which appeared to him completely closed up. Down a narrow street he saw light shining out onto the snow through an open doorway, and he went toward there. A man in a black tuxedo and bow tie was standing by the open door, smoking, and as Joe passed, he glimpsed in at a room bright with red plush and gilt and a few men and women in formal clothes standing around a roulette table.

Joe found his way to a metro station. He stared out into space as did the people he was packed in among. He got back to Oktjabrskoye Pole.

He waited in the blue entrance of the apartment building, huddled against a wall that was scratched all over with graffiti. A couple came out and looked at him, but he looked away to study the box with the buttons, a combination of which would let him into the little inner lobby with the elevator. The couple went out. The door into the lobby was so loose on its hinges,

Joe thought that pushing it, it would open, and he leaned against it, but it rattled without opening. He walked around the entrance, rubbing his shivering body through his clothes.

Abruptly, he went out, without his case, into the snow-filled darkness, but as he was crossing the yard to go out into the street, Zoya came toward him.

She rushed to him and grabbed his arm and said, her eyes wide, "I have been so worried."

Joe laughed. "About what?"

"Please do not joke now. Where did you go?"

"I tried to get onto a train that would take me out of Moscow."

"Out of Moscow? Where?"

"I didn't know. I wanted, all of a sudden, to be in a Russian forest."

Zoya drew him by his arm back into the apartment building, where, in the entrance, was his suitcase.

"You left this here?"

"I left it."

"Where, now, were you going?"

"I was going to look around Moscow for a forest."

"Please do not joke."

"All right, I won't joke."

Zoya pressed the combination of buttons, and when the door to the lobby opened, she picked up Joe's case, her other hand always under Joe's arm as though to support him into the elevator.

She said, "You have bad cold."

"*A* bad cold."

"A bad cold."

She held his arm to bring him into the apartment, which again was very hot.

"Sit, sit," she said, "and I will bring you hot tea."

The sofa was as he had left it, a rumpled mass of sheets and blankets, and after he threw off his hat and coat, he sat, exhausted, in the midst of the mass. As hot as it was in the room, he was shivering.

Zoya returned quickly with a glass of hot tea and gave it to him and said, "Drink it hot," and sat in an armchair to face him. "So you went to train station to get train out of Moscow?"

"I went to *a* train station to get *a* train out of Moscow."

"You thought you could do that so easily?"

"I thought I could, but I found out I couldn't."

"And now, just now, tell me where you were going without your case? You know there is no forest in Moscow."

"I wasn't sure where I was going."

"Drink your tea and then lie down."

The tea was strong and bitter and seemed to cause a lump in his stomach, but he drank it.

"I saw into a gambling parlor," Joe said. "I didn't think gambling would be allowed in the Soviet Union."

"If you belong to the right circle, everything is allowed in the Soviet Union."

"Everything?"

"Everything. You must not just go out to wander in Moscow. Moscow has become a dangerous city."

"Has it?"

"If you are recognized as a foreigner, you will be beaten up and robbed. Do you have money on you?"

"All the money I have in the world."

"You are reckless."

"I guess I am. I'd never have thought that word applied to me, because I've always thought of myself as very careful, but, you're right, I'm reckless. It sure was reckless of me to come to Russia."

"The most reckless you could be."

"I'm glad that I can be reckless. I've always wanted, secretly, to be reckless. Everyone thought I was a good boy, I thought I was a good boy, *you* thought I was a good boy, careful about everything. My parents thought I was a good boy. But I'm not a good boy, I'm reckless. Maybe I'm a bad boy."

"You have a fever."

"Do I?"

"Your fever is making you talk the way you do."

"Then I'm glad I have fever."

"*A* fever."

"A fever," he repeated.

"You must rest."

"Yes, but I want to lie down somewhere where I may never get up, I want to go somewhere so far away, somewhere no one has ever been, I wouldn't be able to come back."

"You must eat something and then you must rest. I will go out and find a chicken in the open market. Not in state-run store, but in the open market I can buy a chicken to boil. And I will buy garlic for your cold."

Joe sat up. "But I don't want to stay here."

"Why not?"

"Whatever my reason was for coming to Russia, it wasn't to be confronted by another American who is everything I left America to get away from."

"But Gerald likes you. Last night, he helped me to undress you and put you to bed. I know he likes you."

"Gerald likes me?"

"He likes you, he likes you. You will stay here, please. You will stay because you must eat and rest, and because Gerald likes you."

Joe fell back among the sheets and blankets. "And you, do you like me?"

"Do you think I would help you if I did not like you?"

"I mean, do you like me as much as you like Gerald?"

Zoya bit her lower lip and stared at Joe for a long while before she answered, "Please understand, I am in such a position that I can only commit myself to people who can help me, and Gerald can help me."

"And I can't?"

"Not in the way Gerald can."

"How is Gerald helping you?"

"By Soviet law I must have job, *a* job. If I don't have a job, by Soviet law I am nonperson. As I, now, don't have a job, I am nonperson. There are many, many of us, every day more and more nonpeople. Soon all of the Soviet Union will be mostly nonpeople, all like ghosts. I had a job. I had a good job, or, in any case, a better than average job at Bolshoi. This meant I was Party member, because if I were not, I would not have a good job. And I am still Party member, so I am Party-member nonperson, because suddenly there was no more work for me at Bolshoi and I had no job. And the state pays me no compensation, so I have nothing to live on. The reason why I don't invite you to my—what shall I call it?—apartment is because I am ashamed for you to see how I live. Gerald gives me money to live, and Gerald promises to get me out of Soviet Union." The thick, black mascara on her eyelids, the only makeup she wore, became wet. "He promises to take me into the West, the mysterious West, from where he comes, from where *you* come. I have got to get out. Here, even as a Party member, I am a nonperson, and I am terrified that everyone here will become a nonperson, I am terrified of what will happen here among our country of nonpeople, of ghosts."

"Gerald will get you out?"

"You undress now and get into bed."

Joe did what he was told, and Zoya wrapped the blanket in its cover around him.

His head on the pillow, he said to Zoya, "And you love him because he will get you out?"

"Love him?"

"Do you love him?"

"If I must, then, yes, I love him."

"Just to get out?"

"How else can I get out?"

Quietly Joe said, "I'll get you out."

Zoya, leaning over him and smiling, said, "You?"

"Tell me how, and I'll do it."

Zoya smoothed his hair. "Do not be reckless. You sleep now. I will go out for a chicken and come back and cook it for you. And please do not go out to look for a Russian forest while I am gone."

Joe closed his eyes.

He opened them to see Zoya carrying a bowl of chicken broth with pieces of chicken and boiled potato in it, and he sat up, the blanket wrapped round him, to eat with a spoon while Zoya watched.

"There must be Americans, from the time of the Russian Revolution, who came to the Soviet Union and started different lives here," Joe said.

"There must have been, idealistic Americans, but if there were any, I don't think there are anymore."

"What would have happened to them?"

"They would have been shot, Joe, if they were lucky, or sent to do slave labor, or to starve in camps."

"For being Americans?"

"For being idealistic. And if there are any left, I think they are trying to find ways to get back to America."

"You think I should go back to America, don't you?"

"I think that you should, unless you came to Russia, not to start new life, but to die in Russia. It is very easy to die in Russia. The nonpeople of Russia do it every day, everywhere, and if they all did it in our forests, our vast, vast forests would be haunted by them."

Joe handed the bowl and spoon to Zoya, and she handed him a handful of peeled cloves or garlic, telling him to swallow them whole.

She said, "You go back to sleep now."

Again, Joe was woken by Zoya, this time with a glass of tea and a large sugar cube. Daylight was showing behind her. She sat on the edge of the sofa and gave him the sugar cube to put into his mouth, then the glass of tea, which he drank through the cube.

Placing her hand over his forehead, she said, "Your fever has gone. The garlic worked. You slept deeply all night."

"You stayed?"

"I wanted to make sure you are well."

"You're right, my fever has gone. I feel better."

"Now you have a bath. There is hot water. Have a bath while there is hot water, because there is no telling when there will not be."

She filled the tub, testing the water with her hand, while he took off his dirty undershirt and underpants. When he was seated in the steaming water, Zoya held a bar of soap and asked, "Shall I wash your back?" He leaned forward for her to soap his back. She said, "Now lie in the water," and he did, and she placed the soap on the rim of the tub for him to pick up and soap his chest and groin while she watched. He felt a deepening sense of comfort with her in the small, smelly bathroom, watching him, naked, bathe. She added hot water and said, "Now stay for a while," and she sat on the side of the bath.

"Now that you are no longer feeling reckless, I will ask you about what you offered to do for me when you were reckless." But she interrupted herself and, smiling, said, "You look too much like boy to have such dark beard. Shall I give you your razor to shave while you are in bath?"

"And my shaving cream."

Kneeling by the side of the bath, Zoya held a small, rectangular mirror out before him when he shaved. When he finished, he asked, "What were you going to ask me about?"

She sat back on her legs. "Will you get me out of Soviet Union?"

Joe rose up in the water, feeling all at once attentive in a way he had not felt in a long time. "If you tell me how."

"Last night, while you were sleeping, I thought about your offer. Did you mean it?"

"Sure I meant it."

"You will do whatever you can to get me out?"

"I will." He sank back so his knees were sticking up from the now gray water and his chin was a little submerged in it. "But I have a condition."

"A condition?"

"That you stop seeing Gerald."

She laughed. "Why do you think I am asking you to help me?"

"So you were with Gerald only because he could help you?"

"Do you think I would have any other reason?"

"You even loved him because he could help you?"

"I would do anything for Gerald because he could help me."

"And that'll stop?"

Zoya clapped her hands. "That will stop."

"He may like me, but I don't like him."

"No, no, I don't like him either, Joe, I don't like him at all."

"Do you hate him?"

"Hate him?"

"I want to know if you hate him."

"Do you need to hear me say that before you will help me?"

"I need to hear it."

"Then I hate him."

Joe stood, dripping, in the bath, and Zoya, her eyes as if seeing not him but all around him, handed him one of those small, napless towels, but it was warm because she had placed it on a steam pipe. And when that was wet, she handed him another.

While, in the living room, he dressed in clean clothes, she brought out the bread and kefir from the day before and sat by him on the sofa as he ate and drank.

She said, "It is not difficult for me to get an exit visa. I can do that by bribing. The difficulty is an entrance visa to any country in the West. The queues at the German embassy of Germans who became Soviet citizens and who want German visas are very, very long, and so, too, are the queues at the Greek embassy of Greeks who, in their civil war, left Greece because they were Communists and came to Russia and became Soviet citizens, and who now want to return to Greece, and the same is happening at the Spanish embassy, where the queues are very, very long of Communist Spanish who left Spain after their civil war and came to the Soviet Union to become citizens and who want now to return to Spain."

"And what's happening at the American embassy?"

"The queues are also very very long there, but of Russians wanting to go to America because America is the country they have all, always, wanted to go to. In all our literature, there are so many characters who want to go to America. And do you know that Lenin, when he was living in Switzerland in exile from his country, thought of giving up everything, giving up the idea of revolution, and going to America?"

"To start a revolution there?"

"Again, you are trying to make me laugh."

"Am I?"

"And Gogol, Gogol, early in his life, in fact tried to go to America, but he was stopped."

"What stopped him?"

"I do not know, but he was stopped."

"I thought he went to the Holy Land."

"Later, maybe because he could not get to America, he went to Holy Land instead."

"Now you're trying to make me laugh."

"The chances of my getting into America, though, are very, very small, unless I know someone. Do you know someone at the American embassy?"

"No."

"No one?"

"No one."

"I know someone at the British embassy, or I know someone who knows someone, but I cannot go ask for myself, I need someone to ask for me. If you do not have someone to speak for you, you stand in the queue for three months at the embassy."

"Three months?"

"You are given a number and told about when your number

will be called up, usually in three months, but if you miss the day when your number is called, your name is crossed off the list, and you must start all over again. When you get closer to the date your number may be called, you go every day and wait all day long in the queue. It is possible to buy days in the queue, one hundred rubles a day. And it is even possible to buy a visa, which is five hundred rubles. But that is a big risk, and most likely you would be turned away by immigration. Most important, you must have a sponsor who will take responsibility of you in all ways when you are visiting his country."

"But I'm American, not British."

"It's not close enough? You both speak English, and England always agrees with whatever America says, so would listen to you, an American. And both countries are in the West."

"You think?"

There was urgency in Zoya's voice. "We can try."

"How does Gerald get people out?"

"I don't know, and I don't want to know."

"Then we'll try at the British embassy."

Zoya stood. "Can we go now?"

"Now?"

"Yes, right now."

"Then, right now."

A light snow was falling through the grayish air, covering in a fine, shifting layer that heavy snow that had fallen and hardened the days past. Zoya, leaving the yard, looked around as if to see if anyone was watching her and hurried along the street. Joe hurried with her to the metro station.

The carriage was empty except for Zoya and Joe and, sitting across from them, a young man who wore wet, torn sneakers without socks, the stained trousers of a pinstripe suit that were ragged at the cuffs, and a dirty anorak. His hair was long and blond and soaked and hung close to his skull and down the sides of his thin white face. His hands were on his lap, crossed at his wrists, and with his head tilted a little to the side, he started out with large blue eyes.

"What is he staring into?" Joe whispered to Zoya.

"He is staring into space."

The British embassy was on the Moscow River, a white-and-yellow, pre-Revolution palace in a compound of both snow and mud. Standing on either side of the gate into the compound were Soviet guards, who, Zoya said, asked to check passports. One of the guards looked carefully at Joe's photo in his American passport, then at Joe, seeming intent on confirming every detail of the photograph in Joe's face. Joe stared at the red star in the guard's visored cap. When Joe was handed back his passport, the guard saluted him. The other guard was still checking through Zoya's passport while Zoya stood stark still, her eyes unfocused. When he handed her back her passport, he didn't salute her.

As Joe and Zoya entered the compound, Joe said to her, "Your guard didn't salute you."

"Of course not. He would never deign to salute another Soviet. It was enough that he let me in, which he would not have done if I had been alone."

"But you have the right to come into the British embassy, don't you?"

"I don't think I do, as a Soviet. In any case, we never know what our rights are."

"Never?"

"We are only told what is wrong for us to do."

They went up the steps of the palace and into the entrance, where there was a built-in reception with a glass panel, and behind the panel a woman with a chignon and a mild face, wearing a cardigan she might have knitted herself. She was English. Joe asked for the person Zoya said was a friend of a friend, and the receptionist smiled mildly and told him to go out and round to the side of the embassy building to the back of the compound, where there was an annex, what had been a garage, and he should go into the garage and ask there. Joe asked her to repeat the instructions, and she did, with her mild smile.

Now Zoya, often swallowing hard, followed Joe down a muddy path along the side of the palace to the back, to the garage. The path led to a door, and Joe opened the door into a large, dim space in which was a small, white trailer with its two windows on one side lit up and before each window a person looking down at two lines of no more than four people each.

Zoya stayed close to Joe when he went to one of the lines. She kept swallowing hard. When he whispered, "This may be easier than you imagined," she didn't answer, but, swallowing harder than ever, kept her unfocused eyes expressionless.

Joe heard, in the line next to the one he was in, an American man inquiring about an entry visa into Great Britain for a Russian woman standing by him, and this made Joe feel, again, a flash of possibility. He simply looked at Zoya to try to communicate to her what he had heard, but she gave no indication of having heard anything, no indication of seeing anything.

He whispered, "Right there, there's an American asking for an entry visa into Great Britain for the woman he's with."

Zoya remained sternly expressionless.

After no more than fifteen minutes, Joe and Zoya stood below a woman with dyed-black hair who looked down at them from the illuminated window of the small, white trailer.

Joe asked for the friend of the friend of Zoya.

Instead of answering, the woman said, with a Russian accent, "Have you been first to receptionist?"

"We went to the receptionist at the entrance to the embassy, who told us to come here."

Her voice raised with sudden temper, the dark, big woman said, "You must first go to receptionist here," and she pointed with a pencil to the back end of the trailer.

Joe apologized, he hadn't known. Zoya followed him to the very end of the trailer, where from behind a small, open window a young, thin Russian woman with natural blond hair looked down at an elderly Soviet couple. The man stiffly handed her a sheaf of papers, which she went through, checking the application forms to make sure they were properly filled out. While the girl was carefully doing this, Zoya, as though she could no longer stand still, wandered away and stayed away until the Russian couple, apparently not knowing where they were going, left with the papers. Zoya again stood still by Joe when he asked the girl for the friend of Zoya's friend.

"She is not here," the girl said. "She has returned to London."

Zoya's face did not suggest any expression.

Joe said, "I'd like to know what I have to do for my friend here to get an entry visa."

"Will you be her sponsor?"

"What do I have to do to be her sponsor?"

"Will you be able to guarantee her while she is in Great Britain?"

Joe lowered his eyes, then, raising them, asked if the friend of Zoya's friend really wasn't there.

"She isn't."

Without saying more, Joe took Zoya's arm and led her, expressionless, away.

Just then, a man left the trailer to go to the back of the garage, where there were the wide doors for the cars. Joe saw him slide back a bolt and open one of the garage doors just enough to let in four people, behind whom Joe saw, massed as far as he could see, hundreds and hundreds of people waiting outside in the falling snow, their pale faces raised to try to look through the partly open doorway into the dark garage.

Outside the embassy compound, Joe and Zoya stood for a while and looked at the Moscow River, running with ice floes on black currents.

Zoya sighed and said, "Maybe the friend of my friend would not have helped."

"Maybe," Joe said.

"And, anyway, she might have been working for intelligence."

"Which intelligence, British or Soviet?"

"You never can tell."

"I'm sorry."

"I see now it was impossible, so there is no need to be sorry. We cannot be sorry for what is impossible."

Joe watched a bare, uprooted tree being carried along the current.

Zoya said, "There is in Dostoyevsky's *Crime and Punishment* the character Svidrigailov, who, just before he shoots himself in his head, says to the man watching him, 'When they ask you where I have gone, tell them I have gone to America,' then he pulls the trigger. Sometimes we say of someone who has killed himself, 'He has gone to America.' "

The uprooted tree sank into the dark water.

"Let us not go back to the apartment now," Zoya said. "Let us walk around old Moscow. At least you will see something you have not seen."

Snow was falling more thinly than before, and sudden, small gusts raised it in swirls from the hardened snow beneath. They took a side street of old wooden houses, in the midst of which was a small church that had been restored. It was painted matte red, and about its bell tower was a row of shining blue and green oriental tiles.

"The state is giving churches back to the Orthodox Church," Zoya said, "and the Church is restoring them. But we do not know if services will be allowed."

"Would you go if they're allowed?"

"Yes, I would go. But not you."

"No."

They went along the narrow street of wooden houses with dirty double-glazed windows. Approaching a wooden, two-story building, which had once been painted white and green and which listed at different angles, with the sign КАФЕ over the door, Zoya said that perhaps they could get tea there, but she told Joe to wait for her to go up the steep wooden steps to see first. She came back down immediately and said, "You must not see how bad a place can be."

Silently, they walked along a curving street of old, yellow houses, in their midst a closed wine shop, and where the curve of the street rounded was the bell tower of another church, this one derelict. A bus, filled with passengers standing close together, passed. Farther along the street, Zoya bought a loaf of bread from a glassed-in kiosk on a street corner, and walking on silently, she and Joe pulled off bits and ate them.

After their long silence, Zoya said, "Gerald will be wondering what I am doing."

"He'd mind if he knew we were together?"

"He'd mind if he knew I tried to get out of the Soviet Union

by going with you to the British embassy. He would know I
am with him only because he can help me."

"How does he help?"

"He helps other women, but I am different, I know, from
the other women he helps, those women I, in our joint venture,
find for him to help. They must pay him for his help. I will
not pay him, because Gerald will marry me to get me out and
to make my residence legal in America."

"Marry you?"

"He has said he will marry me."

They stood at a corner where a young man, to try to keep
warm, was dancing around a glass case in the snow in which
shone a bouquet of red carnations with two lit candles in the
case to keep the flowers from freezing.

Joe asked, "Is he selling those carnations?"

"Yes, of course."

"Tell him I want to buy them all."

"He will ask a lot of money."

"I don't care how much."

Zoya spoke to the young man, wearing a knitted ski cap,
who spoke back, and she said to Joe, "He wants ten rubles for
all."

Joe unbuttoned his overcoat and unzipped his money belt,
from which he took ruble notes that amounted to something
like fifteen dollars at the official exchange note, and he handed
them to the young man, who, frowning, opened the glass case
and presented the flowers to Joe, who gave them to Zoya. The
young man blew out the candles and left with the glass case.

Snow was falling onto the flowers Zoya held.

This feeling came to Joe: if he went to America with her,
he'd restart his life. At twenty-three, he was young enough to

restart his life with Zoya, a life that would be different from any life he had imagined for himself. Zoya would make everything possible.

He said, "I'll marry you."

Her face softened with a smile, a sad smile, and holding the flowers in one hand, she touched his cheek with the other. "Let us return to the apartment."

"To Gerald?"

"To where it is warm."

"Will Gerald be there?"

"He said he would come this afternoon."

"To find out if you have found anyone willing to pay him to get out?"

"Gerald is not demanding. He will not care if I have found no one."

"To see you, then?"

"He said he wanted to see you."

On an impulse, Joe put his arms around Zoya and held her to him, the flowers crushed between them, and he pressed the side of his face against hers.

"What will happen?" he asked.

She drew back a little. "We have a long, long history of suffering here, and I think that what will happen is that we will suffer even more than we have ever suffered. I myself have seen suffering, such suffering that mothers have killed their babies because they could not bear the idea of their babies growing up in such a world as ours. And there will be worse. You can be sure of that. There will be worse." Her tears, black with mascara, reached the corners of her mouth and spread over her lips. "But we must remember, great is our Mother Russia."

Again, Joe put his arms around her and held her for a long while. People in dark overcoats, like large ghosts, passed them.

Now Zoya stepped back and, wiping the tears from her face with a worn glove as she sniffed, said quietly, "Come, we must go back, or you will again catch bad cold."

He put his arm about her waist as they walked to the nearest metro station.

The carriage was crowded, the passengers, as always, standing still and silent and staring out into space. Only one little boy, standing directly in front of Joe and Zoya and holding the hand of his mother, looked up at them, his blond face, with large blue eyes, delicate. Zoya, her bunch of red carnations held close to her chin, looked calm, as if her resignation at being disappointed in not being helped by Joe at the British embassy, in not being helped by Joe in anything, were complete. Joe could do nothing for her, and she accepted that he could do nothing for her, but, Joe knew, she didn't blame him for this. It made her closer to him. She looked at him over her flowers and smiled her sad but completely resigned smile, and she whispered, "He is a beautiful boy. We say, as beautiful as a girl. Too beautiful for this world."

When they got out of the metro into the still-falling snow, Zoya said, "We won't go back to the apartment now."

"Supposing Gerald is waiting?"

"But you said you did not want to see Gerald."

"Yes, but if he is waiting."

"Waiting in that apartment? Why should he be waiting?"

"I just wondered, supposing he's waiting?"

"Why do you care if he is waiting?"

Joe hunched his shoulders.

"Maybe you want to see him," Zoya said, "because he wants to see you."

"No, no."

"Come, I will introduce you to a friend."

Zoya took Joe along back streets, the snow on some of them hardly marked by the tires of passing cars, and along trodden paths through snow-covered, empty lots, all about them, at different angles, cement apartment buildings. They went to an apartment building with a broken outside door and the stoop missing, so Joe had to jump with Zoya over the gap into the entrance hall, which looked like a dank, dark, dirty cellar made of cinder blocks, the walls covered with graffiti in pencil and chalk. The door into the lobby of the apartment building was also broken in. Down an unlit passageway that smelled of grease and boiling cabbage, Zoya knocked at a door that was unpadded, its wood unpainted. A thin woman, wearing spectacles so thick they made her black eyes appear minute in her gaunt, pale face, opened the door. She was Alla, and she spoke English as if she had spent her life in an English-speaking country, where the English was a mixture of British and American, as was Zoya's. Alla had a number of gold-capped teeth. She didn't seem surprised that Zoya had brought Joe, but took his presence, as she must have taken everything Zoya did, for granted. She said, "Come on, come in," and opened the door wide on a room for which she made no apologies.

Handing her the large bunch of flowers, Zoya said, "This is gift from my friend Joe."

"Thank you, Joe, but I have nothing to put them in but an old cooking pot."

"Better than a hole in the ground," Joe said, trying to joke, but feeling how much he couldn't joke.

The apartment consisted of one room, a kitchen, with a corroded sink with a dripping tap, and on a wooden shelf above the sink were chisels and hammers and screwdrivers, and above these was a large primitive painting of peasants gathering sheaves of wheat. Beneath the sink was a terra-cotta bowl of potatoes. The floor was covered in linoleum so worn it was difficult to make out what the pattern was. Beyond the sink, on either side of the room, were two divans, which had knitted blankets folded on them, and at the end of the room was a dresser with one leg missing and on top a gas ring and above it black and battered aluminum pots hanging from nails in the cracked wall. Alla put the flowers into one of these pots.

She said, "No Westerner has ever been into my flat before. I am glad to show you how we live. Most Soviets would be too humiliated to show you how they live, as my friend Zoya here. I am not humiliated, I am proud to show you, proud to show you what we are reduced to in our country, proud to show you how our country is falling apart in all its details, proud because everything you see proves that I have been right about our country, that we have destroyed ourselves. I am a very proud person, and especially proud to be right."

"Alla is always right," Zoya said to Joe.

"Of course I am." Swinging out her arm as if indicating a vast, comfortable room, Alla indicated the two divans facing one another across the narrow space.

Zoya and Joe removed their shoes and put on misshapen felt slippers and sat on one divan, which sank with broken springs.

Alla said, "All I can offer you is tea, stark black tea without sugar or milk or anything else."

At the dresser at the back of the room, she boiled water in a pot and talked nonstop about the shortages. After she poured the boiling water into a teapot, she turned to Joe and asked, "Are you a Western liberal?"

He laughed.

Alla was bringing the teapot and three enamel mugs on a painted tin tray to the divan. She said, "If you are, and if you came to our Soviet Union because you wanted to be among like-minded liberal people, you have made a mistake. The only people in our Soviet Union who have your liberal views should be shot." She put the tray on the divan across from the one Joe and Zoya sat on and poured out the tea and handed out the mugs. Then she sat on the other divan, her legs crossed under her. "Let me tell you, honestly, what I think of people from the West, idealists from the West, who come to the Soviet Union believing in the ideals of Communism—I think that there must be a few good, well-meaning people among them as there must have been a few good, well-meaning people among the Nazis."

"Alla," Zoya said with a shocked voice.

"If Joe is an idealist, as good and as well-meaning as he no doubt is, he should be shot."

"Alla, Alla."

She made a gesture to Zoya to shut up. "But, Joe, if you came to our Soviet Union to commit suicide, then you have not made a mistake. There is no other reason to come to our Soviet Unon but to commit suicide. You are in the right country for that, because we ourselves have committed moral suicide, all of us, by joining the corrupt though we know they are corrupt, the corrupt who are, oh, such idealists. To save ourselves, or so we thought, we joined the corrupt. And we tried to forget they are corrupt. And now, to save ourselves, we join the more corrupt, and we try more than ever to forget they are corrupt. We have only ourselves to blame for our suicide, and no one from outside should feel sorry for us. I want to tell foreign businessmen *not* to invest in our Soviet Union. I want to tell people from outside, this is *not* a country to be loved, but to be despised for being an utterly false country. I want to tell people from outside to use our country in whatever way they want and to get whatever they can from it and not to feel guilty if they think what they are doing is destroying our country, because our country is already destroyed by our own hand, and the guilt is all ours."

"Aren't you scared that the KGB will know what you say about your country?" Joe asked.

Alla made a gesture as of throwing the whole of the KGB out the window. "I have always spoken as I do now, even when I was trying to save myself by being as corrupt as any of the corrupt and telling myself I wasn't. I never got into trouble because *they* knew I wasn't advocating the overthrow of the government and didn't deal in the black market. *They* considered me nothing but a raving intellectual, someone who didn't matter. And now it matters even less what I say. I will teach you a good Russian expression. Listen and repeat. It is all *damiato*."

"Alla," Zoya said.

"It is a very good Russian expression, which you will hear more and more often."

"*Damiato*," Joe said.

"Good," Alla said.

Joe felt Zoya's hand reach for his and grasp it.

Alla said, "You will stay for something to eat. I have only potatoes, but I have a lot of potatoes. We can eat as many boiled potatoes as we want, and I have salt. Salt and matches are still available, just, and if you parcel them out, there's no telling how long we will be able to live on salt and matches, salt to eat and matches to keep warm."

Joe dropped Zoya's hand. "Zoya, I think, may be concerned about getting back to the apartment."

"I am not concerned," Zoya said to him. "But you, I think, are."

"If Gerald is waiting—"

"You'll stay here with me," Alla said.

Joe smiled a little at her. "For you to pass judgment on me?"

She returned his smile with a wider one. "I will have to know more about you first."

"Have you been to the West?"

Alla shook her head. "Why should I go and be poor in the West? I am not beautiful enough for anyone in the West to be interested in me. Being in the West wouldn't teach me any more than I already know here about being poor."

Joe asked Zoya, "You really think it's all right to leave Gerald waiting?"

"You are too concerned about Gerald," Zoya answered. "I don't understand. It is as if you *want* to see Gerald."

Alla asked Zoya, "How are things with Gerald?"

"I try not to think."

"I admire Gerald," Alla said. "I think Gerald has the right attitude toward the Soviet Union now, the only attitude any foreigner with some money should have, which is to come and take advantage of our collapse in any way at all, selling us drugs, pornography, guns, buying our icons for nothing and smuggling them to Helsinki and selling them for what would be for us vast fortunes, making us pay to get visas into Western countries that may not be valid. We deserve to be exploited, deserve to be punished. No other country in the history of the world has failed as we have failed, and though I do not believe in God, which all good Communists do, we deserve the harshest punishment of God."

"That can't be," Joe said.

"Ha. Ha." Alla got up. "Now I will boil potatoes."

"We will help peel them," Zoya said.

Alla drew the large terra-cotta bowl of potatoes between the divans and next to it set a pot of cold water and an enamel basin for the peels, then gave Zoya and Joe knives. Alla talked nonstop, about how she had heard there had been, a few days before, an explosion in a factory outside of Moscow that released a cloud of poisonous pollution, about the general pollution of land and rivers and lakes everywhere in the Soviet Union, and holding up a potato, said, "As a matter of fact, these very potatoes are filled with nitrates."

Zoya said, "Please, Alla, enough."

Alla laughed. "Enough? We don't know the half of it."

And yet, with all this talk of the disaster around them, a sense of intimacy among them deepened in the dim light from a lamp on the dresser at the end of the room.

As Alla was draining the pot of boiled potatoes into the corroded sink, the door to the apartment, just behind her, opened and in came a boy. Alla smiled at him, but Zoya jumped up from the divan to rush to the boy and embrace him and kiss him.

"Yura, Yura," she said.

Yura drew back from her and smiled. His sideburns weren't cut square by a razor, but ended in points, so he must not have yet shaved, if, given the fairness of his complexion, he would ever shave. His blond hair covered the tops of his ears, and Joe saw, when the boy turned his head away for a moment to say something in response to Alla, that the hair at his smooth nape ended in a point. Alla seemed to be telling him to stay and eat with them.

Zoya grabbed the boy to her again and, laughing, spoke in Russian, and the boy laughed with her. Then Zoya, holding his chin, asked him rapidly many questions in Russian, to which he answered over and over, "*Da, da, da.*" It was as if she had asked him if he'd been a good boy.

Yura's blond face was made broad by his cheekbones. His

nose was straight, and fine, Asiatic folds of flesh were at the inside corners of his blue eyes. He was as beautiful as a girl.

Zoya brought him by his hand to meet Joe, and the boy bowed his head a little when he held out his hand for Joe to take.

The boy said something in Russian, which Zoya, still holding his hand, translated. "He is sorry he does not speak English."

Joe said, "Tell him I'll teach him some American expressions, all he has to know to get by."

Zoya told him this, and the boy, smiling a wide curve of a smile with his lips closed, told her something, and she said to Joe, "He wants to learn one now."

"Always walk backwards to get to where you want to go."

Zoya translated for Yura, whose smile curved in a greater curve, but he didn't laugh, and Joe thought, from his sad eyes, that he perhaps never laughed.

Alla came toward them with a bowl of boiled white potatoes, which she placed on a stool Yura brought from the back of the room, then Alla sprinkled salt over the potatoes and gave each person a fork.

Zoya told Yura in Russian to come sit next to her, on the other side from Joe, and when he did sit next to her, she again hugged him and kissed him and told him endearments in Russian.

Alla said, "There is talk of whole areas of Moscow not being heated. If people freeze to death, that will be the solution to the housing problem."

"Please, Alla," Zoya said, sticking out her bottom lip. "Let us not think about such things now."

"Eat, eat," Alla said. "I'll make more tea to drink."

With an ever deeper sense of their intimacy, the talk sometimes in Russian and sometimes in English, with Alla or Zoya to translate to Yura what Joe said or to translate to Joe what Yura said, which was mainly about ice hockey, they ate the potatoes with their forks, then lounged back on the divans. Alla lay lengthwise on hers. Zoya, between Joe and Yura, put her arms about Yura and cuddled him to her, almost rocking him in her arms. They were silent, and in the silence Zoya hummed what sounded like a lullaby and Yura closed his eyes.

Looking at them, Joe said softly, "He has fallen asleep."

Yura's head was on Zoya's shoulder.

Zoya said quietly, "There should be two worlds. One world would be for people who will do anything to live in this world, which means doing anything to make money, because without money you can't live in this world. And other world should be for people who are not interested in making money."

"What would they live on?" Alla asked.

"Whatever, it would not be money."

"So they wouldn't have to eat or wear clothes or live in houses?"

"No, they wouldn't."

"That really would be another world," Alla said with a light laugh.

"I always think how strange it is that to live in the world requires having money. It *is* strange, isn't it, Joe?"

"Yes."

"I'm afraid it isn't at all strange," Alla said.

Zoya said, "Why is the world the way it is and no other way? Why, I am always asking myself, is this without the possibility of being another world? This causes panic in me, real panic, so that I sweat as if I have a bad fever. I think, 'Nothing can be different, nothing can be different,' and I go crazy, hallucinate, again as if I have bad—a bad—fever, about some place that is different, as different as can be. And why can't that place be where we all live, why? My panic gets bigger and bigger the more I can't understand why what should be so easy can't be, just can't be. Why? We are learning now about the horrors that happened in our Russia, that may again happen in Russia, about the thousands, the millions of people pressed into slave labor, about the vast, vast mass of silent women and men going to work in the forests, the mines, to dig canals. But I keep saying to myself, 'Why couldn't Russia be different?' It has to be possible. To keep sane, I have to believe it is of course reasonable that the world can be different. I think it is only the sense that it is possible for the world to be different that keeps me alive. If I stopped believing that, I would die. Sometimes I think I am close to it. My belief in possibility just manages to hold itself, by I do not know what willfulness, against the certainty that nothing will be or can be, ever, different, and that the world will destroy itself."

"It will," Alla said.

"I know it will, but willfully, I believe it won't. What do I mean when I say I want to imagine something that has never before been imagined, greater than all the most positive images of a new world, the vision I grew up with and believed in, as my parents believed in it? Was it such a lie? Was it? If I can't say what it would be, that world, if it is unimaginable to me, how can it be a lie? How can the unimaginable be a lie? That's what I want the unimaginable to be: so different we *can't* imagine it, and because we cannot imagine it, it can never be a lie. And that must be God."

"You're crazy," Alla said.

Zoya rocked the sleeping Yura. "I once tried to live a totally different life, a life that had nothing to do with my past life. After I had to leave my job, I tried to live, as many young people must now try to do, without money. I was not as young as most of them, the small group I belonged to. There were ex-soldiers from the war in Afghanistan in our group. We thought the only way to live without money is to live in a monastery, to live religious lives in a monastery. We went to a monastery in Vologda region. The priest who let us in didn't like me, I didn't know why, and he separated me off to stay with old, old women. But I managed to see my friends, managed to meet with them, out in the forest. Some had drugs. One ex-soldier, who was an addict, had serious drugs. I watched him inject himself in his arm, and after he finished, I said to him I wanted to inject myself. But the syringe broke when I tried to inject it. So I sucked the drug from the syringe. I spent a terrible, terrible night in the forest, terrible. And so, too, the ex-soldier, who committed suicide that night. Next day, I found none of our group. I went into the church of the monastery to pray, and I saw the head priest standing alone, there at the gates of altar screen, and as I went to him, he held out his hand for me to kiss it. Maybe he knew what happened the night before in the forest, maybe not. He held out his hand, and he was smiling, and I thought, 'All right, he doesn't hate me, he separated me from others because he knew it was dangerous for me, a woman, to be with those others, who were children.' I knelt before him and he held his hand closer to my lips and I bit it, I bit his hand. He left me and I stayed in church all day, lying flat on floor, and prayed, and in evening I left the monastery."

After a silence, Alla got up and said she would make more hot tea.

"We must go," Zoya said. "As soon as Yura wakes up, we must go."

"But he may sleep like that for the rest of the night," Alla said.

"Then I hope he does."

Joe said, "Gerald—"

Frowning a little, Zoya said, "Please do not mention Gerald now."

As she looked at him, Joe leaned forward and for a moment pressed his forehead against Zoya's shoulder on the other side from the one Yura was sleeping against.

A sudden sob broke from Zoya and she shouted, "I cannot anymore, I cannot, I cannot."

Startled, Joe drew back and Yura woke and also drew back, blinking. Zoya grabbed Yura to bring him back to her, but he, still blinking, held back, wondering what was happening. Zoya put her hands on the sides of Yura's face and spoke to him in Russian, and as constrained as his head was, he nodded to everything she said. Maybe she was telling him to be a good boy. Yura stood.

Quickly she got up and said to Joe, "You are right, we must return to Gerald."

But Joe lay back heavily on the divan.

"Now you don't want to go," Zoya said.

Joe rose slowly. Standing, he reached out a hand to shake Yura's, but then, instead, he reached out and held the boy's head and kissed his forehead. When he let the boy go, he turned away immediately for his hat and coat.

At the doorway, he said to Alla, "You haven't yet passed judgment on me."

"You are not quite as bad as you think you are," Alla said.

"Thanks."

On their way in the snowy darkness, Zoya and Joe didn't talk, and when one or the other bumped slightly into the other along the narrow paths, they pulled back, as if the awareness of one another's proximity kept them apart rather than together.

In the entrance to the apartment house, Zoya took Joe's hand and pressed his index finger on the buttons of the box that would open the door, and as she did, she said out loud the numbers of the combination.

He asked quietly, "You want me to know the combination so I can come back if I go?"

"I want you to be free."

And after Zoya opened the door to the apartment, she gave the key to Joe.

Joe looked in and saw a dim light and stepped back, imagining that where the light was, Gerald would be, waiting. And as he followed Zoya through the small entranceway into the big room, he anticipated, with an expectancy that frightened him and that he wished would pass but that held some part of him, seeing Gerald in an armchair, a glass of vodka raised in his hand to salute them, smiling. But there was no one.

Snowflakes hit against the glass at the end of the room with a faint ticking sound. Gerald had been here, or someone had been here, and lit the dim wall lights, and had gone, and in the absence of Gerald, or of someone else, there was only the sound of the snow falling against the glass.

While Joe stood in the center, Zoya walked about the room as if to make doubly sure no one was there. Then Zoya came up to Joe, and he, without speaking, took off her hat and threw it on an armchair, then drew off her gloves and threw them on the armchair, then unbuttoned her suede coat and lifted it from her shoulders and drew it down her arms and, as it fell, gathered it up and threw that, too, on the armchair, and he carefully unfolded her gray scarf from about her throat. She sighed deeply as he drew her to his body, hot beneath his overcoat, and kissed her; and as he held her, she pulled off his hat and unbuttoned his coat to press herself closer to his body. She slipped her hands around him under his coat, and he put his hands on her long neck, tilting her head a little from side to side, to kiss her.

As she made up the sofa, he undressed in the warm apartment, then got under the bedclothes and watched her undress. In the silence of the room was that continuing deep sense of the absence of someone, and Joe and Zoya would make love in that absence. He lifted the bedclothes for her to get in beside him.

But the moment he felt her body all along his, he knew that he wouldn't be able to make love. He held her to him and kissed her, kissed her forehead, cheeks, neck, but how could he tell her that he held her and kissed her, not to have sex with her, but for something else? How could he tell her it wasn't sex with her or anyone else that he wanted, but something beyond that perhaps had nothing to do with sex? Weeping, he kissed her face, over and over, until her face was running with his tears. All the while, she spoke softly to him in Russian, running her hands through his hair.

When she said, "Oh, my love," his sobbing broke into a high, long wail from deep in his lungs, and he cried out, "Oh God, help us."

But Joe did not believe in God.

NINE

*When he'd been a boy, he had always run away from the wan-
derer, who was sometimes invited into the kitchen by the cook and
given food. Now a young man, he was one afternoon walking
along a hedge on the prince's estate and was startled to see the
wanderer lying in a ditch on the other side of the hedge, and about
to turn away he was stopped by the wanderer's rising and staring
at him over the top of the hedge, and he returned the wanderer's
stare.*

"You have traveled a lot around the world," he said.

*"I have," the wanderer answered, "and what I have seen
makes me sure that the world will cease to be the world we know
and become a different world."*

"What world?"

"I don't know."

"Does anyone?"

The wanderer stared more deeply into the young man's eyes

and said, "Come with me," and moving slowly because of the chains he wore under his ragged clothing, he walked toward the edge of the forest along a boundary of the estate.

The young man followed the wanderer into the forest, past high, interconnecting mounds of moss with mushrooms growing out of the mounds that looked like a range of hills that the young man, a giant, looked down on; trickles ran down the hills like rivers, and ants herded together on them like black sheep. When the young man looked up into the dimness streaked with light, he imagined he became very, very small and he was looking up from the roots of grass and cow parsley and burdock into blades and stems and leaves. There was no path, and often the wanderer had to hold branches aside with his staff to let the young man go through. They went through a crag and came into an open space surrounded by high rocks, and in the middle of the space was a big oak tree.

The wanderer made a gesture for the young man to wait, then went, with a slowness not caused now by his chains, to the tree. He seemed to speak to it. He raised his hand for the young man to come.

The trunk of the tree was hollow, and a naked man was standing in the hollow. His long hair was matted about his body, his shoulders and chest and thighs, so he looked as if he were a hairy creature. The bark of the tree had grown over the opening of the hollow, and he was visible only through a slit. He would not be able to get out if he wanted to. When he raised his hands, his fingernails, some curved like horn and broken and jagged, caught at his hair, and his white, wrinkled flesh was exposed. His face was smooth, though, and his eyes clear, and when he looked at the young man through the slit in the tree, he smiled.

The wanderer said, "He is the saint of the monastery even

deeper into the forest and has been here longer than you have been alive."

The man in the tree made a gurgling sound in his throat.

The wanderer said to the young man, "You can ask him any question you want."

The young man asked the saint, "Will there be a different world?"

"Yes."

"And what will it be?"

The saint rolled his eyes up so only the whites showed, and his voice sounded like running water. "It will always, always be beyond you to imagine."

TEN

Waking, Joe saw sunlight streaming through the dirty glass door at the end of the room, and sitting in the sunlight, almost invisible in it, was Gerald, who seemed to have been there for hours, looking at Joe sleep. All Joe could make out clearly of the big man was his smile.

Pushing himself up by his arms, Joe was about to ask, alarmed, "Where is Zoya?" as if her absence was due to Gerald's presence, as though he had come while Joe was asleep and sent her away. And if he had sent her away, Gerald had remained for a severe account from Joe of what she was doing in bed with him. But Joe knew that Zoya had left shortly before he had fallen asleep.

From his almost invisibility in the dust-filled sunlight, Gerald said, "I waited for you and Zoya yesterday with food."

"I'm sorry."

"No need to be sorry. I ate it all myself—black caviar,

smoked sturgeon, bread and butter, and a bottle of vodka, from a hard-currency shop. And what did you eat, boiled potatoes?"

"Yes, at the place of Zoya's friend Alla."

"I thought as much. I like Alla. What did you think of her?"

"I liked her."

"Was her son there?"

"Is Yura her son?"

"Isn't he? You can never know, here, how people are related to one another. Families as we know them seem hardly to exist." Gerald said all this in a monotone, without moving, as he appeared not to have moved in hours. "And I presume you came here after your dinner of potatoes and Zoya went to her apartment."

"I came here, but I didn't ask Zoya where she was going."

"I doubt she went to work, though she could have. What time was it?"

"Ten o'clock, around."

"She could easily have gone off to do some work at that time, though I sometimes think Zoya is less professional about her work than I am, and I am, I must say, disgracefully unprofessional."

"Not knowing what the both of you do, I couldn't say."

"I suppose you'd like to know."

Joe sat up and pulled the bedclothes about himself. "I don't know if I would."

"Right. . . . I brought you some breakfast."

Joe thought his cold, with a fever, had returned. Wrapping the bedclothes closer about his body to contain his nakedness, Joe, still partly asleep, said, "Thanks." He knew he must try to be attentive to everything Gerald said and not take what he said for granted. Gerald always meant inwardly something other than what his words meant outwardly. His constant smile when he spoke showed that.

Joe thought, Gerald must know Zoya spent the night here, but can he know, too, that nothing happened? It seemed to Joe that Gerald did know.

"Get up and shave and have a bath and do whatever else you have to do before you dress, and then have breakfast," Gerald said. "I'll wait. I've been blessed all my life with not caring about waiting. In fact, I love to wait. It is a kind of blessing, waiting for someone else, because it relieves you of having to do anything else but wait."

"I'll hurry."

"Don't hurry."

Joe didn't want Gerald to see him naked. He clutched the top blanket in its cover about himself and with a free hand grabbed some clothes from an armchair and rushed to the bathroom, and there he did take his time shaving and bathing, always aware, though, of Gerald in the other room. He came out of the bathroom wearing creased and limp clothes, but with his face shaved and washed and his hair combed. He felt his insides were trembling as if he had a low fever.

Gerald was sitting where he had been, the sunlight thick with dust. Pointing to the desk, he said, "In that bag there you'll find good bread, a jar of apricot jam, instant coffee and milk, and some bottles of Cuban fruit juice. If you'd care to, you could set out a charming little breakfast on the coffee table before your sofa. You'll find plates and cups and glasses and knives and such things in the kitchen."

In the kitchen, Joe found the garlic Zoya had bought, and he peeled and swallowed three cloves. The kitchen, with a cement floor and a bulb hanging from the ceiling with a shade burnt on one side, was dirty. Joe gathered together what Gerald had asked him to and went back to the living room, where Gerald had moved to one of the armchairs near the coffee table, and he appeared as though he had been there, immovable, for days and days. Gerald, wherever he sat, always appeared to have been sitting there, immovable, for days and days. He was wearing his polo shirt with the stretched collar and his tweed jacket.

Twiddling his long, thick fingers, he said to Joe, "Set everything out there nicely for our breakfast," and Joe did as he was told.

"You didn't bring hot water for the instant coffee," Gerald said.

"I'm sorry."

"Come to think of it, I didn't ask you to, so there's no need to be sorry."

In the kitchen again, which smelled a little of escaping gas, Joe heated water in a blackened kettle on an old gas range, then brought the kettle out, steaming.

"I've put the coffee into the cups. I like doing what I can. All you need do is pour in the water."

Joe once more did as he was told, then sat on the sofa. He had no appetite, but thought he might vomit.

"Now have some fruit juice, all the way from Cuba," Gerald said. "Imported fruit juice from Cuba may be the last product the Soviet Union does import from there, but the importation won't last long, and Cuba will be the only country in the world trying to remain Communist after all the others have given up. It's actually terrible fruit juice."

Joe opened a small bottle with a torn and dirty label and drank it down, and when Gerald, as if concerned about Joe's well-being, told him to drink another bottle, he did. He was thirsty.

"Now take a piece of bread and cover it with lots and lots of apricot jam," Gerald said. "Don't stint on the jam. I myself won't have any breakfast."

As Joe swallowed, his stomach almost rejected the food, but he drank coffee to keep it down.

"I've been looking forward to seeing you again."

"Can I guess why?" Joe asked, trying to joke, as he thought Gerald would want him to do.

"You can try."

"You want to know things about me."

"Do I? I think you're presuming a lot. What could I, who already knows everything about everyone, want to know about you?"

"You want to know if I like jerking off into girls' panties."

Gerald liked that and laughed an abrupt laugh. "No, that wouldn't interest me enough. Try again."

"You want to know if I like shitting on a woman's bare tits."

"Even better, but no, not yet interesting enough to me. Try again, though."

"You want to know if I lied and Zoya came here last night and we fucked."

"I like you, I really do. But, I have to tell you, my interest in you doesn't have quite so much to do with you in yourself as you might imagine."

"I don't understand that."

"I can of course tell you what I think of you, if you're interested, which I think you are."

"No thanks."

"Give in, boy, give in. You are interested. Don't hold back.

You hold back, so far back you seem to be useless to do any-thing. But think of what you'd be able to do if you gave in to hearing what I think about you, which you want to hear. Every-thing you've repressed in yourself would make you vital, and you'd be doing what now you can't even imagine yourself ca-pable of. It doesn't take much to give in—just the risk of being, oh, ridiculous. Is it in you to be ridiculous?"

"I'd like to think so."

"And do anything, but *anything*, and not care what anyone, but *anyone*, thinks of you?"

"Maybe, yes."

"Or maybe not. Maybe something holds you back so much there's no way you can give in, holds you back so much you're made useless by it. And what is that something? I could tell you, but I want you to ask me to tell you. I'm not referring to any kind of justification for what you are, because I'm sure that you, like me, have a loathing of justifying excuses, such as that you are the way you are because of something that happened to you when you were a boy that was so terrible it excuses what you are now. I'm sure nothing terrible happened to you."

"No, nothing terrible happened to me."

"What did your father do?"

"He was a local building contractor."

"He built your family house?"

"He did."

"And you spent a happy childhood in it."

"I did."

"And your parents weren't rich, but not really worried about money, and they were pretty much happy together."

"They were."

"So you don't have any excuse for being the way you are."

"No, none."

"You have a girlfriend?"

"I had."

"And nothing terrible happened between you so she's no longer your girlfriend?"

Joe said abruptly, "No."

"Nothing you want to talk about."

"There's not much I want to talk about."

"Unlike me, you mean. I like to talk about everything."

"I know."

"You wouldn't say if anything happened to terrify you in all your life?"

Joe laughed. "I think only what I was able to imagine."

"Oh, I don't doubt that in your helplessness you're a person of the most vivid imagination. Do you want to tell me what a bad boy you are in what you imagine?"

"No."

With a burst of laughter, Gerald said, "I like that, I like a person denying that even the horrors of what he imagines can justify his being the bad person he is. The worst kind of Nazi is the Nazi who did terrible things during the war—helped lock a whole Russian village into their church and set fire to it so the people burned to death—and who tried, after the war, to find some way to excuse what he did, or worse, even, try for some kind of reparation. Not that I don't believe in forgiveness. I believe in forgiveness, totally absolving forgiveness, as long as the sinner doesn't try to excuse his sin, but just says, 'I did this, I did that,' with no expiating explanation of what he did, and certainly with no idea that he can make right what he did wrong. I'd forgive a man who said, 'I killed my girlfriend with an ax,' but I'd take back that forgiveness, I'd condemn him for being a fake, if he tried to justify what he's done." Gerald yawned. "But this is getting so boring. Why do I go on? I don't want to. Is it because you want me to go on?"

"Maybe."

"You won't give in, however much you want to."

"Give in, so the bad boy I am will finally become the bad man you are?"

"That's good. You *do* have wit. You do, you see. Work on your wit, your detachment and irony."

"I'll try."

Gerald pursed his fat lips, thinking. "If you won't admit you're interested in talking about yourself and what I have to say about you, let's talk about me, which I'm sure interests you as much as it interests me. Frankly, I'm only interested in you insofar as you're interested in me, if that doesn't sound too candidly egocentric." Gerald settled more, never to move, in the chair. "Tell me, do you really think I'm a bad man who can't be anything but bad? Tell me what you think of me."

This stopped Joe's thinking, and he looked at Gerald's smiling mouth for a while before he asked, "Tell you what I think of you?"

"Yes."

Joe slowly ate the bread and jam, drinking coffee with milk from time to time, and didn't answer Gerald's question.

Gerald smiled more. "Do you think someone as bad as I am can be helped?"

"Helped, how?"

"Oh, say, by someone else praying for him."

"Praying?"

"Yes, praying."

Astonished, Joe tried to laugh. "If you're asking me, I don't know what I'd pray for if I were praying for you."

"No?"

"I'm sorry, no."

"Don't be sorry. I don't like people to be sorry. I'm never sorry. No doubt, anyone praying for someone like me wouldn't know what to pray for."

"No doubt."

"Do you ever pray, boy?"

Joe tensed, then after a long time said, "I did lie to you about my coming back alone here last night and Zoya going off somewhere else, to her apartment or work or wherever."

"Did you?"

"We stayed and we fucked."

"You did, did you?"

"While we fucked, she told me everything that you and she do together when you fuck."

Gerald half lowered his lids. "And did that excite you?"

"I was hoping she'd come up with something I hadn't heard of before that you and she do together."

"You are not a good boy."

"No."

"And you like being a bad boy."

"Oh, I'd like to be a bad man."

"Like me?"

"Maybe like you."

"The first thing you've got to learn about being a bad man is that bad men don't lie. Bad boys lie, but not bad men."

"What do bad men do?"

"They always tell the truth."

"You think I lied to you about Zoya and me?"

"As what you said was, in its way, so flattering to me, I really would like to accept it as the truth."

"But you know it isn't?"

"I know that Zoya would never risk fucking another man, however less repellent he is to her than I am, because she knows what's invested in me."

"You trust her."

"I don't trust her. I have a hold on her. Did Zoya tell you I promised to marry her to get her out of here?"

"She did."

"Do you think I'll do it?"

"No, I don't."

"That's great. That's the kind of talk I like to hear, without your saying you're sorry for saying it. That's being a man. What do you think I'll do with her if I don't marry her?"

"I'd have to know you better to say."

"You already know me well enough. Tell me what you think I'll do with Zoya if I don't marry her. Come on, tell me what you think of me. You don't want to hear me say what I think of you, but I'm passionately interested in what you have to say about me. Not that I care what anyone thinks about me, but I am interested in knowing. Do you think I'll abandon Zoya when I find someone else even younger and prettier who'll fuck me for a promise of marriage to get her out of here? Do you think I'm that kind of person, or even worse? Do you think I'm a totally worthless person who can never, ever be saved by anyone praying for him? You do, don't you?"

"I didn't say that."

"But you think it. I'm not drunk now, and when I'm not drunk, I'm afraid I take myself rather seriously, rather, but not too seriously. You think I can't be saved, don't you?"

"Is that what you want me to say?"

Gerald laughed, then wiped his mouth with the back of his hand. "You're not going to give in, are you? You're not going to let me tell you about yourself, and you're not going to listen to what I think of you, and you're not going to tell me just what you think of me, not going to tell me the truth about myself. You want to, I know you want to, because you know that hearing the truth and telling the truth would make a real man of you."

Joe sat back on the sofa. "You tell me more about how bad you are."

"Oh, as for that—did Zoya tell you what our business is?"

"She said you helped people get out of the Soviet Union."

"People she finds for me, because my Russian isn't good enough."

"She said she helps you find people."

"Women, all young women, all girls. Though I suppose they could be boys, too." Gerald scratched his head. "You know why, don't you, just looking at me? Because there's a demand for girls and boys as prostitutes in other countries, and because so many Russian girls and no doubt boys want to fulfill that demand. They're common in every country in the West now, in France in the Bois, in Italy along the *autostrade*, in London advertising themselves with calling cards stuck in telephone booths. They are particularly common in Tel Aviv. It's like after the Revolution when White Russian women who had to escape or be killed, women of the best families, became prostitutes even in China. What do you think of me for doing that? Do you think anyone praying for me will save me? Do you think there's any help for me?"

"No."

Gerald laughed a loud, harsh laugh. "I really like you, boy. I do, I do. You don't know what you might have risked if you'd said yes. You don't know how angry I can get. Anyone tells me there's help for me, anyone tells me I can be saved, and I go into a rage, and in that rage I'm not responsible for what I do."

Joe put both his hands over his mouth.

"Did you ever have religion, boy?"

"Yes," Joe said through his hands.

"So you did pray once."

"Yes."

"What was your religion?"

"Catholic."

"Catholic? From where I come from, we don't consider that a religion but a damnation. I had religion, too, once. I had to go to church with my pa the senator and my ma the senator's wife to our church in Washington, and every time at church I heard about somebody being saved, a rage would come over me. And you know why? Because I knew it was a lie. I knew no one was going to be saved, not me, not my ma or pa, not my brothers and sisters, not my grandma and grandpa, not even Aunt Emma, who was justified if ever there was anyone justified." Gerald began to speak in a Southern accent, maybe from one of the Carolinas, Joe couldn't tell. "I didn't want to be justified, I didn't want to be saved, not me, and I was so irreverent my ma and pa and my aunt and everyone in our church not only gave up on me, they were glad that I was out every night at parties where I could be as irreverent as I wanted because I made people laugh, and that was an advantage in Washington. But you don't have religion now?"

Joe dropped his hands from his mouth. "No."

"And what made you stop having religion? You want to tell me. Tell me."

Joe tried to sound ironic, but talking from the side of his mouth, he knew that he didn't sound ironic. "Well, let me tell you, then—I guess I realized that religion made no difference to me or, for that matter, to the world." He felt his face go red.

"When did that happen?"

Joe could do nothing now, his face redder and redder, but to go on trying to sound ironic, and he twisted his lips to talk even more from the side of his mouth. He was sure Gerald's only interest in him was to ridicule him, and that was all right with Joe, except that Joe wasn't up to responding to the ridicule as he wanted to. "You really are interested."

"No, I'm not really, but you are in telling me."

"All right, all right, I'll tell you. I stopped having religion when I stopped being able to fuck."

"Ah, now I know you're telling the truth. You can't fuck?"

"No."

"Let me tell you, no longer being able to believe because you can't fuck seems to me a banal excuse for giving up religion."

"You said it before—I loathe excuses."

"I'm disappointed in you, boy. There must be a real reason for your giving up religion."

"If there is, I don't know it."

Gerald's eyes went out of focus. "I sometimes tell myself there has to be a real reason why I gave up religion." Then his eyes all at once focused on a spot on the coffee table, in the midst of the breakfast things, as though something had just appeared there that amazed him. "Where's the bottle?"

"The bottle?"

"There was a bottle of vodka standing right there in the middle of that table."

"I don't think there was."

"There wasn't? I didn't bring along a bottle of vodka? Go and look in that plastic bag I brought the breakfast things in, there on the desk, to see if the bottle's in it."

At the desk, Joe held the limp bag upside down. "Nothing."

"Where'd it disappear to, then? I know I put it on the table."

"I don't think it was ever there."

"Are you telling me I'm hallucinating? Look around the room, boy, get down on your hands and knees and look under the furniture. I'm not accusing you of hiding it, but I want this room searched."

Joe got down on his hands and knees and glanced round. "Nowhere to be seen."

"I'll be damned, just when I was getting into our conversation and needed a drink to keep it going."

Joe now stood before Gerald.

"I don't know if I remember your name, boy, but that doesn't matter. I like you, and I was enjoying our conversation. But to continue I need a drink, or two or three. Now, if I give you the money, will you go out to a currency shop and buy a bottle?"

"You don't have to give me any money."

"I insist."

"Just tell me where to go."

"There's a currency shop in the National Hotel. Take a taxi there and back. You can always get a taxi if you pay in dollars. Hurry up, now, because I may lose the thread of what I was going to say."

Out on the street, a taxi stopped as soon as Joe held out a hand, which meant the driver knew he was a foreigner, and when the driver said, "Five dollar," Joe said, "*Da.*" Many cars were parked outside the National Hotel, with drivers sitting in them, waiting for foreign passengers, and among the cars were the prostitutes.

Joe didn't go into the hotel. He wasn't going to buy a bottle of vodka for Gerald and go back to the apartment and listen to Gerald talk.

For a while, he watched the girls walk among the parked cars, tall, slender, beautiful girls with silk scarves that were folded into their coats, then he turned away.

He went down into an underpass, along which people stood at small tables selling badly printed magazines. When he came out, he found himself in Red Square, where sunlight was shining on snow. As he went toward the red-and-black granite mausoleum of Lenin, he passed a small wedding party, the long white veil of the laughing bride blowing sideways in the wind. Behind the bride was a girl in a pinafore, with a large ribbon tied in a bow at the top of her head, laughing, too, as she helped the bride to hold the blowing veil. A line of people was on the right side of the mausoleum, waiting to go in. Joe stopped at a distance and watched them go in, slowly, and he couldn't make himself go on and join them. He looked up at the brick walls of the Kremlin, at the pointed towers with the red stars, and he could not get himself to go any nearer to the mausoleum, at each side of the closed main doors of which stood guards of honor.

He turned back to descend into the underpass, where an old woman standing at a folding table was selling badly printed holy cards. Joe noted that there were girls, and boys, too, loitering in the underpass, and he thought they must be prostitutes.

The commissionaire opened the door of the hotel for Joe, who walked into the lobby and followed signs along corridors with threadbare runners to the currency shop. He bought a large bottle of vodka and at the checkout counter saw a little cardboard box of lapel pins of the head of Lenin.

He did not want to go back to Gerald, he thought, and he wouldn't go back to Gerald, even though he had bought the bottle of vodka. But he didn't know where he would go.

Leaving the hotel, he saw, among the parked cars, Zoya talking with a girl who must have been a prostitute. Joe stepped back, but Zoya, as if she were expecting him to appear, turned to him. He waited for her to come to him, her breath steaming about her in the cold, bright air.

He said, "Gerald asked me to come buy him a bottle of vodka."

"You shouldn't have come out. I see your fever has come back."

"How do you see it?"

"In your eyes."

"I came to buy this for Gerald because he more or less demanded that I should, but, just now, I was thinking I wouldn't go back to him with it. I bought it with my own money, so I don't owe him anything."

"If you don't go back, where will you go?"

"That's what I asked myself."

"Come, we will go into hotel for you to have some hot tea."

But the commissionaire, who had opened the door to Joe, wouldn't let Zoya in.

"Please do not insist," Zoya said. "It is too tiring. Wait here." She quickly went back to the prostitute she had been speaking to, who had remained standing among the parked cars, spoke briefly to her, and returned to Joe. "We can walk, and that will warm you up."

Joe wouldn't ask Zoya why she had been talking to the prostitute, but he didn't know what to ask her, and she seemed not to know what else to ask him. They walked up a wide boulevard, Ulitsa Gorkogo, to Pushkin Square, of yellow and white neoclassical buildings and the statue of Pushkin in the center of the square, all under brilliant snow.

Joe said, "I want to ask you again if you will you marry me."

Zoya shook her head. "I must marry Gerald."

"Must?"

Zoya pressed her lips together, then after a moment said, "I am not free."

Joe smiled a little. "To marry a boy?"

"I do not like men, but men are necessary."

"And boys are not."

"Please."

"I'm sorry. I suppose I must get back to Gerald with this bottle of vodka."

"Must?" Zoya smiled.

Joe smiled.

"No, don't go back. We will go to Alla's. Yura will be there. Yura told me this morning when I saw him how much he liked you and how much he wanted to see you again."

"Where did you see him?"

Zoya raised a shoulder and let it drop to indicate that she might have seen him anywhere.

"No, I think I really must get back to Gerald."

"Bring him the bottle, then come to Alla's, where I will be, and Yura."

"You think it'll be that easy to get away from Gerald? He'll want me to pour out his drinks."

"He is capable of pouring out his drinks alone."

"He'll want to talk."

"He is capable of talking alone."

"What should I say to get away from him?"

"Tell him you have a date."

"That's all?"

"Gerald respects privacy."

"I'll come after a while."

"Come while there is still sun. Soon the sky will cloud over and the sun will go and there'll be more snow. Will you come?"

"I'll come."

"You will go back to Gerald by taxi, so let us walk back to the hotel for one."

As they walked back down Ulitsa Gorkago, they were again silent. Only when Joe was in the backseat of a car and Zoya was standing outside holding the door open did she ask, "Will you tell Gerald you saw me?"

"If you don't want me to, I won't."

"You can tell him."

"He'll understand?"

Zoya winced a little. "He'll understand." She shut the door and the driver turned on the ignition, but she opened the door again, and after she spoke to the driver in Russian she told Joe to get out of the car for a moment because she wanted to tell him something. They walked away from the parked cars. She said, "You know, prostitutes in Moscow around the big hotels used to work for KGB, some of them. Not anymore. Now they work for Mafia. Though how much is KGB and how much is Mafia, how can we know? I will tell you what I should not tell you—I used to work for KGB. Though I no longer am KGB, how much am I still in contact with KGB and how much with Mafia, how do I know? My privileges are all gone, but I am still in contact with people, and this is how I help Gerald. You were wrong to come to this country. It is a terrible country, always was and always will be, and everyone in it, including myself, is bad."

"Bad?"

"Yes, I am bad. Now go back to Gerald."

But before Joe got into the car, Zoya grabbed him and kissed him. "Come as soon as you can to Alla's. Yura will be waiting. He told me to tell you he will show you his Russia."

"His Russia?"

"He has his Russia."

In the car, Joe touched the palm of his hand where it had been kissed by Zoya.

ELEVEN

The young man went with his father the bailiff to inform the old prince that the village zemstvo was now Soviet.

"Good," the prince said, "good."

"They will be coming to tell you, you must leave. They will no doubt take away the estate and do what they will with it."

"Good," the prince repeated, "good."

Then the bailiff said to his son, "Now tell us about the bear."

"The bear?" the old prince asked.

The young man said, "This morning, walking around the estate for what may be the last time, I came on a bear's lair in the snow."

The prince sat up. "A bear hibernating on my land. I used to hear stories when I was a child of such things, but from generations and generations back. A bear on my land." The prince smiled. "We'll go draw it early tomorrow morning."

"The sooner the better," the young man's father said.

"You mean, before the bear is killed by my new masters?" The prince sat back. "I have never, ever killed a bear, and I would have once thought it impossible that I ever would, impossible because I am and always have been against hunting. And now I want to kill this bear."

In the morning, when the young man and his father got to the prince, they found him with his old valet—older even than the prince—who was cleaning the prince's carbine, which the prince, his hands trembling, was not capable of doing.

At the entrance to the ravine, the horses were stopped and the men got down from the old shooting car into the snow and put on their snowshoes. The young man's father attached the leashes to the dogs and was pulled forward by them, ahead of the others, through the ravine. When they got to the end of the ravine, facing the snow-covered clearing, the Samoyeds strained at their leashes and began to tremble. On the other side of the clearing was the bear's lair, and over it hung a thin cloud of steam.

The prince said, "We must get closer."

The young man's father told him and the valet to go ahead, carefully, and put up a snow butt nearer the bear, and the two trudged over the snow, wooden spades on their shoulders. The old valet was quicker in throwing up the snow butt than the young son of the bailiff. Then the prince, his carbine at the ready, and his bailiff, his carbine on a strap over his shoulder and pulled as before by the Samoyeds, took positions behind the butt.

Nodding at the Samoyeds, the prince whispered to the young man's father, "Slip their leashes."

The bailiff slipped the leashes on the Samoyeds and then made the sign of the cross.

The two dogs held low, their mouths wide open, their fangs and gums exposed. One of them bounded ahead of the other, then the first raced ahead to the bear's lair. They jumped round and round the mound of snow, advancing on it and retreating, snarling. From time to time, one of them would stop short and bite its rump, then, as if it momentarily forgot what it was doing, would stare at the lair, then, remembering, would begin again to worry the mound. These pauses seemed to make them aware that they were ridiculous, and their ferocity was to try to convince themselves that what they were doing wasn't ridiculous. The mound of snow didn't appear to be at all worried.

The prince said to his bailiff, "Call the dogs back."

Astounded, the bailiff asked, "Call them back?"

"Yes."

"I don't think I can. I don't think they'll come."

"Call them."

The bailiff, frowning, stood and called. Surely, the prince knew the dogs couldn't be called back. The dogs stiffened and went still. The bailiff called them again. But, gone still only momentarily to recollect something they had forgotten, they after the moment sprang at opposite sides of the mound and with frenzy dug at the snow. A great black paw swung out from the side of the mound and struck one of the dogs so it fell back with a high yelp. The dog returned to the mound while, on the other side, the second dog continued to dig crazily. The whole mound rose, rose and cracked and broke into pieces that fell from the black bear rising onto its hind legs, and growling so the sounds of the dogs seemed far away. The bear knocked one of the dogs to the side, where it lay in the snow shuddering and bleeding from a wound in its chest, then the bear turned to the other dog, fell to its front paws, and advanced on it as the dog leapt forward, its teeth bared, to bite into the bear's neck, but the bear, slowly and heavily, sat back and swung at the dog with such force it flew into the air and dropped, its back broken. Whining, the dog tried to crawl away.

The prince, trembling, raised his double-barreled shotgun to *sight the bear, who simply remained standing on his hind legs. Slowly, the prince lowered the carbine. Sweat was running down his face. Everyone watched the bear, who was motionless. And then suddenly the prince raised his gun and shot and the bear raised its arms out wide and then folded them in, and fell sideways.*

TWELVE

EVEN AS HE APPROACHED THE CEMENT APARTMENT with the bottle of vodka in a plastic bag, Joe thought that he didn't *have* to go back to Gerald. And when, in the entryway, it occurred to him that he had forgotten the combination of numbers that would let him into the lobby, he thought he couldn't go back to Gerald, and he'd go instead to Alla's, where Yura, and maybe Zoya, would be waiting for him. But the inside door was partly open, and all he had to do was push it to enter the lobby. And when he got to the cement landing, outside the brown vinyl–covered door to the apartment, all he had to do was ring the bell. Here, too, he thought he wouldn't ring, he'd go away, because he didn't want to see Gerald again. His arm seemed to reach out of itself and ring the bell.

He heard no one coming to the door inside and thought that Gerald, unwilling or unable to wait any longer, had gone out for a bottle himself. Relieved that seeing or not seeing

Gerald was no longer a decision Joe had to make, Joe turned away. With his back to the door, however, it opened.

He heard the big man shout, "I hate waiting."

Turning round to him with a forced smile, Joe said, "I thought you like waiting."

"I hate it. Give me the bottle."

Gerald's hands were shaking. There out on the landing, he pulled at the bottle to get it out of the plastic bag but only twisted it in the bag, which, finally, he tore at furiously so the neck of the bottle would stick out. He unscrewed the cap, and spilling vodka as he poured it, he filled the cap as a jigger and slugged it down, then repeated this twice more. He seemed to become immediately drunk and, losing his balance, leaned against the door, which swung open with his weight so he lost his balance even more, and Joe had to reach for his shoulders to steady him.

Gerald used the cap yet again for a jigger he slugged down, then, blurry eyed, he looked at Joe with that expression of not knowing who he was, and also, whoever he was, of disdain for him—disdain because Joe was not Joe but a human being who, like all human beings, was to be despised.

That this big, drunken man should see Joe not as individually but as universally disdainful in some crazy way reassured Joe, reassured him and amused him.

Staggering, spilling vodka from the bottle that still had the plastic bag twisted around it, Gerald went into the living room and let himself fall backward into an armchair.

The sky had clouded over and the light in the room was dusty gray.

Filling another cap with vodka, his hands now steadier, Gerald said, "While you were away, I tried to keep the thread of what we were talking about and I kept losing it. It was such an interesting conversation. What were we talking about?"

Joe, his hat and coat off, sat on the sofa, which was as he had left it, the bedclothes in a mess. "I don't remember." He told himself he shouldn't have come back, he of course shouldn't have come back, but should have gone to Alla's.

"Try to remember," the big man said.

"I really can't remember."

"You're not interested in our conversation. I see you're thinking of something else."

"I have a fever."

Offering him the bottle, from which he tore off the twisted plastic bag, Gerald said, "Have a drink of vodka for your fever."

"No, thanks."

"You won't drink with me?"

"No."

"Instead of being insulted by your refusing to drink with me, I'm going to take it as a compliment. You want me to have the entire bottle to myself. Now, that's a reassurance, having a whole bottle to yourself. And look"—Gerald raised the bottle and sloshed the liquid inside—"I've only just emptied the neck."

Though it was hot in the apartment, Joe pulled the blanket around his shoulders.

Gerald said, "It's not your fever. Whatever you're thinking of, it worries you. You're worried, aren't you? Why?"

"No reason."

"Tell me. Tell me what you're worrying about."

"About Zoya."

"About what will happen to Zoya?"

"Yes."

Gerald waited a moment, then asked, "About what I'll do to Zoya?"

Joe pulled the bedclothes more closely about his feverish body, all the insides of which seemed to him to be trembling. He looked at Gerald, then looked away with great boredom at the very sight of the man.

Gerald said, "You want to save Zoya from me, is that it?"

"I guess Zoya can save herself if she wants."

"I'm not so sure of that. Save herself how in this country?"

Joe's boredom made his voice go slack. "I wouldn't know."

"No, you wouldn't, because you don't know this country the way I do." Gerald swigged from the bottle, then wiped the back of his hand across his chin where the vodka had dribbled. "Ah, this talk makes me suddenly remember what we were talking about so interestingly before you left. We were talking about being saved."

"Were we?"

"Show some interest, boy. This is important. I was brought up with the belief that there is nothing more important in a man's life than that he be saved. I heard that over and over and over, until I couldn't stand it. But, you know, I still hear voices from my past telling me, telling me, telling me that I've got to be saved. Are they the voices of the singing, hand-clapping nigras I was taken from time to time by my father the senator and my mother the senator's wife to hear in a nigra church, for I never knew what reason? Because those voices of singing, hand-clapping nigras could get to you, boy, could get to you even though you would only hear them, would only be in the midst of nigras, at their church, and those voices would get you all the more because you didn't really know what you were doing in that nigra church. Don't get me wrong, boy. I don't have no longing to be back in such a church, oh, no. If I miss anything from those days, those days when I had religion because my parents had to have religion, because it was policy for them to have religion, though I didn't know this, though I thought my parents went to church, went even to the nigra church, because they believed that by going to church they would be saved—if I miss anything, it's the attention I got, even from nigras, because my father was a senator and my mother the wife of a senator. But the fact is that once upon a time I did believe, I did, that we could be saved. Do you ever hear voices?"

"No."

"I think you do. But, given as you're Catholic, the voices would be calling you, calling you, calling you to damnation."

"I don't hear any voices."

"You do, but you just don't want to listen to them. And I understand that, because I don't want to listen to my voices. And what made me change, what made me change from the boy who had religion, who believed we could all, even and maybe especially nigras, be saved, to the man who realized that religion is a lie, that no one will be saved, and that the truth is politics, which saves no one? What turned me from being a good boy into a bad man—if I ever was a good boy, which I doubt? Maybe it was not anything terrible, but the simple fact I found that there was so much fun to be had in politics, in getting so much attention, in being invited to all the parties, in being social, and that there was even more fun in making fun of the attention, of the parties, of all the society that laughed at my ridiculing it, and that the greatest fun was in telling the truth. Were your parents social, boy?"

"No."

"I expect not, being Catholic."

"Maybe you've forgotten that the USA had a Catholic president."

"That doesn't mean he was *accepted* socially."

"I wouldn't know about such things."

"Just as well that you don't, so you don't know if you're in or not."

"I don't think I've ever been in."

"That can't hurt you unless, like me, you know you're out. So where was I? Wondering how I lost religion. It was not because of anything terrible that happened to me to make me realize there can be no God, but because I had more fun not believing in God, because I found the truth that none of us will be saved allowed me to be ironical and witty and even cruel, whereas the lie that we can be saved allowed me no irony, no wit, no cruelty, but insisted that I must be serious. I hate serious people. Do you?"

"Yes."

"But you're serious."

"Only when I'm alone."

"I'm serious, too. Don't you think I'm serious?"

"No."

"I'm glad you said that. I would have gotten real angry with you if you said I'm serious. How can anyone be serious who knows he can't be saved? How can anyone seriously think he can be good if he can't be saved? What I've wanted to do, you know, is be so bad that I'd be beyond being saved, just to get rid, finally and forever, of those voices telling me no matter how bad I am, I can be saved. I've tried to be so bad that the voices stop because they realize I've gone too far and can't be saved. I've gone very far to convince those voices I know they lie, so they'll stop. If you can convince the voices that you know that they lie, they'll stop, because they themselves know they lie. The truth, which makes men of boys, is that no one will be saved, that we're all bad."

"Are we?"

"A rhetorical question, that. All you want to hear from me is how bad we are. Let me ask you, boy: Did you ever try to help someone?"

"Yes," Joe answered in a slack voice.

"Who?"

Joe shrugged.

"And what happened?"

"I failed."

Gerald smiled. "You failed?"

"Yes."

"And the fault is?"

"You tell me."

"Yours."

Joe lowered his eyes.

"I admire you. I can imagine you being tempted to tell yourself that, really, you didn't fail yourself, the world failed you, as surely as the world fails boys, and girls, and women and men, every day, everywhere, fails them politically, ideologically, religiously. But you know that blaming the world is just finding an excuse, a cheap excuse, for your failing, all your failings. And you hate excuses, hate them as much as I do. Like me— who has never blamed any failing on anyone but himself—you will, finally, always blame yourself instead of trying to find excuses for your failings in the world."

Joe raised his eyes. "I saw Zoya."

"You saw her at the National?"

"Yes."

"Working?"

"I suppose she was working."

"Zoya could do it all on her own, you know. She doesn't really need me. Anyone looking at me would see right away that I'm no real help to anyone, not anymore. I even get thrown out of cheap cafés on the Arbat because they look at me and know I'm not the kind of customer they want, and this in a café where all you can get is black tea and slices of stale white bread. But Zoya thinks she needs me, thinks that without me . . ."

"She won't get out?"

"You really worry that I won't be good to Zoya, don't you?"

"Should I worry?"

"Oh, I think that maybe you have some reason to worry. I'm not going to marry Zoya, you were right. But I am going to get her out. I'm going to get her out with me, and wherever we go, she'll be mine, just mine, more mine than if we were married. And when I said I mean she will be mine, I mean she will be *mine*. And that means you've got plenty to worry about Zoya for."

"You think Zoya needs you so much that once you get her out she won't leave you?"

"She won't leave me. Listen to this, boy, and tell me what you think of me after. Once we're out, I am going to sell beautiful, sexy Zoya. You do find her beautiful and sexy, don't you? She *is* beautiful and sexy. Let no one tell you that life is not worth a plugged nickel. The life of a beautiful, sexy girl is worth a fortune."

"I don't believe you."

"You don't believe me?"

"No."

"I tell you, men do not lie. I'm going to get Zoya out and I'm going to sell her to anyone who'll pay the fortune she's worth. You don't think I'm capable of that? And, believe me, if Zoya killed herself when she found out what I'd done, I would only feel that I should be comforted because I'd lost out on a business deal, I would only want to be wept over because I'd be left a penniless vagrant in a world that doesn't give a fuck about penniless vagrants."

Joe sneered and stuck out his lower lip.

"You know I'm capable of it, don't you? You even expected something like this of me, didn't you?"

"You won't do it."

"Are you testing me, boy?"

"You're testing me."

"Maybe, but you like being tested. Tell me, boy—don't you miss anything from your religion?"

"No."

"No chanting, no candles, no incense, no dark niches with half-hidden statues of saints in the shadows?"

"No."

"Not the whip and the crown of thorns, the hammer and nails, the cross—all, I've been told, so meaningful to Catholics?"

"I don't think you have any idea of what it is to be Catholic."

"Isn't it Catholic to press your forehead to the crucifix and, grieving for the world, pray?"

With a little moan, Joe turned away.

"What did you say?" Gerald asked.

"Nothing."

"You said something."

"I didn't say anything."

"You told me you don't pray, but if I sold Zoya to be raped and tortured and slowly, slowly killed, would you pray for me then, pray for me even though you know your prayers can't possibly do anything at all?"

"No."

"No?"

"No."

"You wouldn't pray for me?"

"No."

Gerald held the bottle between his thighs and coughed so his face went purple. Still coughing a little, he said, "Just as well, boy, just as well, because if you ever got down on your knees to pray for me, I'd kick you in the teeth, I'd knock your head off, I'd stamp the life right out of you. And that, I tell you, I can do."

Joe stood. "I've got to go."

"I'm not stopping you from going anywhere you want, boy. If you've got to go, you go. I won't even ask where if you don't want to tell me. But, before you go, tell me what you think would be just enough for me to do to Zoya that would get you saying the smallest prayer for me?"

"Everything you say comes only from your drunken imagination."

"You think?"

Joe went for his hat and coat.

"You go. I presume you're not going out to meet Zoya, because she said she'd meet me here this afternoon. You go, and I'll stay and wait for Zoya."

Joe dropped his hat and coat. "I won't go."

"You should go. You have a date. I'm not going to ask who it is you've got a date with, because you may not want to tell me. In any case, I want to be alone with Zoya when she comes, so I want you to go on your date. I'll make Zoya happy. You go out now and make the person you're meeting happy."

"I'll wait with you for Zoya."

"No, no, you go."

Joe walked up and down the room.

"You really don't want to know what I think about you, boy?"

Joe went to a wall and pressed against it.

"I'll tell you anyway. I'll tell you the real reason why you failed religion. The real reason is that you are too bad to have religion. I think that all you need is the slightest flash of self-illumination to realize everything you are, even in your own naked body, is bad. That's what you want, that flash of self-illumination, just the slightest, because just the slightest would be enough to make you see fully what you already see almost fully. And I'm just the person to cause that flash. You know I am. That's why you don't want to leave me and go on your date. You want to get that flash from me."

Facing the wall, with its blue wallpaper patterned with golden medallions, Joe said, "I don't want to leave you because I don't want Zoya to be alone with you if she comes."

"That's a weak excuse. You want to hear me talk about your being bad, don't you? You want to hear the worst, don't you? You want to hear the worst about the whole world, about the whole bad world we live in. You want to hear about what's most terrible in the world, what kills all the good people who can't take the terrors of the world."

Joe turned away from the wall and quickly grabbed his hat and coat and put them on as he left the apartment.

Behind him, he heard Gerald shout, "Listen to me, boy, listen. You want to be on the side of the bad men and the killers who have renounced comfort and commiserating tears as unworthy of them, and who make no excuses."

On the landing outside, Joe leaned against the closed door and shut his eyes.

THIRTEEN

*The man was at a meeting in the clubhouse in the Siberian for-
est—a shack made of wide, knotty planks—and he sat on a bench
among his comrades, listening with attention to the comrade foreman about their project, which was to clear a wide area of the
forest, then dynamite the earth, then build a great furnace, stoked
with trees cut into damp logs, to run the steam-driven bores that
would descend deeper into the earth to determine the depth of the
water that they would then dig down to.*

*They started digging in the summer. Just before winter began,
they reached a depth that required the sides of the crater to be
reinforced, and for a month, the men watched from above a pile
driver sink steel piles, with earth-shuddering blows, around the
inside of the pit, and deeper than the pit, wedging them in tightly
against one another to form a massive iron drum. The man stood
about on a raw hill of dug-up earth and stones and looked down*

*into the pit. The day he went back down into the pit, snow began
to fall.*

*The digger next to him struck his spade against a stone and,
scraping it clear with the edge of the spade, called to him, in the
midst of sounds of pickaxes and spades, "Hey, comrade, who would
have expected to find a stone so far down?" A number of men
circled round the stone. They gave way only when the comrade
foreman came and seemed about to give a speech, but he only
reached out to take a pickax from one of the men and, swinging
the pickax under the boulder and thrusting his weight against the
handle, dislodged what had been where it was from the beginning
of time. He didn't have to give a speech, as his actions did it for
him: there was nothing man could imagine that would not be
realized.*

*The man, a month later, was the first to shout out as he dug,
"Mud!"*

*Then all the men, with the help of pumps to suck up the water,
began to dig through the mud. Their boots were always deep in
the black, thick wash. About the round wall of the pit silt oozed
through the cracks between the steel piles, however tightly they
had been wedged. Cigarette smoke at that depth hung thick and
still in the air. Now, the sound of the pumps made it impossible
to talk, and the men in the pit worked silently in the light of small
electric bulbs suspended from long wires.*

*Slowly, piles in the round wall began to bulge inward, then
suddenly great clots of silt fell between the piles into the pit.*

Someone roared, "Comrades!"

*Throwing down their spades and pickaxes, the men all together
hefted a metal beam and tried to prop the bulge to keep it from
swelling further. But the lower end of the beam was sinking into
the silt, and planks, spades, pickaxes, even, from some men, jackets,
caps, and boots, were thrown into the mud to keep the beam from*

sinking. Again and again, the beam sank into the black slime. Old truck tires hung around the wall as bumpers, and these the men pulled down, and while some workers, their muscles straining to bursting, raised and lowered the end of the beam, others wedged the tires under it. When the end of the beam was placed down into the midst of the tires, it held, and the top pressed against the bulge in the pile with enough force to keep it from buckling farther. But the silt, with a constant, heavy, dark flow, continued to pour into the pit and rise above the boots of the men to their knees. The pump was unable to cope with the load, and more pumps were brought and orders screamed out above the men's heads in the high dimness, hung with rising and lowering gondolas and illuminated by bulbs that began to flicker. As the silt poured in, it became more watery and might soon start to splash in. Reinforcements of men were lowered into the pit in the gondolas, so there were so many men digging away the silt left by the pumps they hardly had room to swing their spades.

Among them, the foreman shouted, "Comrades, for the love of God, save our great Soviet Union!"

While some men dug, others wedged thick planks into the opening caused by the bulge to try to stop the flow of silt. The planks were flung out by the force of the pressure behind them, and one, flung out, hit a worker in the head and killed him. The foreman shouted for the pit to be abandoned, and men began to jump into the gondolas, so many that some of the men had to hang on to the cables as the gondolas rose. Then the power failed, electric lights went out, and the gondolas, packed with men, stopped, swaying in space.

The man was left in the pit with other men, all watching, with passive wonder, at buckling and twisting piles that gave way to great gushes of mud as dawn light began to show in the vast round of the pit opening high overhead.

FOURTEEN

Snow was again falling from the low, darkening sky as Joe hurried along the paths he tried to remember that went to Alla's apartment. Zoya would be there, would be waiting for him with Yura, and he'd tell her not to go to the apartment where Gerald would be even drunker than when Joe had left him. He'd tell Zoya never to go to Gerald again.

Half running along a path diagonal across an empty space among the apartment houses, he realized he was going in the wrong direction, and he ran back along the path to find the right one. Just at the angle where the right path went in another direction from the path he'd just ran back along, he stopped, panting.

Everything Gerald was capable of imagining suddenly struck Joe as being of the flattest banality.

He ran along the path to the almost derelict building in which Alla had her apartment and where he would find Zoya

and Yura. He jumped over the gap in front of the outside doorway, pushed open the flat wooden door, and rushed down the
corridor to the door of Alla's apartment. He knocked. Yura
answered, smiling.

Yura exclaimed, "Joe!" and then he went on in Russian to
say something Joe thought he had been told, maybe by Zoya,
to tell him, though if by Zoya she would have known that Joe
wouldn't be able to understand Yura's Russian.

"Alla?" Joe asked.

"*Ally nyet.*"

Joe asked, "Zoya? *Gde Zoya?*" but he didn't understand
Yura's responses, except Yura's repeating, over and over, "*Da,
da,*" and nodding his head. Joe became frightened that Zoya
would not appear, but was perhaps on her way to Gerald, was
already there. He hoped that whatever it was Yura was telling
him, with animation and sudden flushes in his clear, blond
cheeks and forehead, had to do with their going out to meet
Zoya, because he seemed to be saying that they would go out.
He made this emphatic by putting on his ski jacket and ski cap.

Yura, excited, hurried ahead of Joe, eager to get to where
he wanted to show Joe something, and Joe followed him to the
metro. In the station, Yura took from his pocket the kopeck
pieces for the turnstiles. Joe saw in Yura's large, big-knuckled
hand, held between thumb and index finger, a five-kopeck brass
coin, with the world superimposed on the hammer and sickle
and surrounded by sheaves of wheat and surmounted by a star.
Then Yura dropped the coin into the slot and Joe went
through.

In the train, a young woman, with blue eye makeup that
almost formed circles around her blue eyes, looked at them
intently, then away out into deep space.

On the street again, Yura continued to rush ahead of Joe,

often turning round and signaling to him to come more quickly. They were among high-rise apartment buildings with large letters and numbers painted on them; Kb 59–109. Yura took Joe into one.

In a glassed-in booth under the stairs of the entrance, a woman was knitting. She was sitting, one leg folded under her, on a built-in bench covered with thin pillows in different flower patterns, and tacked on the wall behind her was a cloth, hanging in folds, of yet a different pattern of flowers. The skirt of her dress was of a pattern of flowers different from all the other patterns, and so was her kerchief, tied tightly round her head and knotted at her nape. She was the concierge. She didn't glance up from her knitting as Yura and Joe passed her to go up the stairs. On the landings were galvanized buckets of sand against fire.

With a key, Yura opened a door padded in brown vinyl, beyond which was another door, wooden, not locked. Yura pushed it open and held it for Joe to go in first, into a narrow hallway with closed doors on all sides. On hooks along the hallway were coats and hats, and under them collapsed boots. Pushed against a wall was what had once been a drop-leaf table, the drop leaf gone, and on it was a big jar of onions in vinegar. Yura helped Joe off with his coat and hat and hung them up, took off his and hung them up, then, opening another door, brought Joe into a small, square room, on which he shut the door.

The room was papered with old maps of countries and cities, and among these were pinned colored snapshots of groups of people, all young, in an apple orchard, the branches sagging with heavy fruit, and Joe wondered if such photographs appeared in every Russian apartment. There was a sofa and a table made from the drop leaf from the table in the hallway set on wooden boxes, and a large wooden spoon on it. A big ward-robe, with dusty suitcases on top, was standing partway into the room, half hiding an unmade bed behind it.

Joe stood in the middle of the room while Yura walked back and forth before him, speaking as animatedly as ever.

"Zoya?" Joe asked.

"*Da, da. Zoya.*"

Joe grabbed Yura by his shoulder to stop him from pacing so excitedly, and the boy stood, silent, surprised and expectant, facing Joe.

"Yura." But Joe didn't know what else to say, wouldn't have known what to say if Yura understood English. It wasn't to find out what they were doing in this room, what they were waiting for, as if where they were and what they were waiting for didn't concern Joe.

The light in the room was becoming dim as the light outside dimmed more and more with falling snow.

"Yura." Joe felt a sudden weakness in his arms and legs.

Yura understood when Joe asked for the toilet and showed him, out in the hallway, a narrow water closet with a seatless, brown-stained bowl and a pile of torn-up newspapers by it. The cistern high on the wall and the pipe down were corroded. Joe vomited.

Going back into the small, square room, Joe saw Yura sitting still on a wooden chair by the window, a shadow against the disappearing outside light. Yura's head was lowered. He didn't hear Joe, who stood at the threshold. When Joe entered the room, the boy didn't rise from his chair, but remained with his head a little lowered, and now Joe paced back and forth.

He hadn't closed the door to the room and saw a door off the hallway open into a lighted room, and an old woman, with a hair net and an old, open-worked crocheted bed jacket and black stockings and black felt slippers, come out to use the toilet, then go back into her room and close the door.

As Joe continued to pace before Yura, the boy watched him, frowning a little. Joe said, as though he were calling him from a distance, "Yura." The boy got up and came to him in the darkening room. In a low voice, Joe said, "I want to die."

Yura laughed, and suddenly a yellow ceiling light was lit.

"Larissa," Yura called. At the doorway to the room was a girl, like Yura about sixteen, who, as she came forward, shook her head and combed out her long blond hair with her fingers. Strands fell over her face, and she pushed them aside. Yura, excited again, introduced Joe to Larissa.

As Yura had, she assumed, matter-of-factly, that Joe could understand Russian. From time to time, she paused and puckered her full lips together so her cheeks became long hollows and her delicate cheekbones stuck out more prominently, and she looked at Joe with a lowered forehead. When she spoke, she did quickly, having given a lot of intelligent thought during her pauses to what she said.

Yura was stepping from foot to foot, like a dancer restless to dance, but he didn't speak while Larissa did, or even during her pauses. All he did was hold out his arms, one toward Larissa, the other toward Joe, about to put them around their shoulders and bring them close together, as if he wanted Joe to have the same relationship with Larissa as he had, whatever that was.

But then, the way Larissa spoke to Yura seemed to leave Joe out. He didn't mind being left out, but liked watching the two young people, she, as with the authority of a dance instructor, telling him what he must be attentive to in his dancing, while he, entirely attentive, frowned a little. Whatever they were talking about, she knew more about it than he did, and he listened with the awareness that she knew more, that he had everything to learn from her. It was as though he, in his simplicity, counted on her to tell him what to do, and she, protective as much of his simplicity as his talent, took him on as her responsibility. Joe watched them more closely, her talking rapidly then pausing and pursing her lips and brushing strands of blond hair from her pale face, and he, his slightly oriental eyes blinking slowly, as attentive to her during her pauses as when she spoke. She said something that made him smile, and when he smiled, she smiled, too, and together they laughed light, bright laughs. Joe felt a pang at the sight of these two beautiful young people in clothes that didn't fit them, her skirt too big for her and her blouse too small, the collar of his old dress shirt frayed, the trousers of a pinstripe suit worn at the cuffs, his belt that of a much bigger man but drawn in tightly, with holes punched into it for the buckle, about his waist. In their way, whatever way that was, they were in love with one another, maybe in the way that made her love him for his boy's innocence, an innocence that precluded sex, and made him love her for her woman's knowingness, a knowingness that included the worst horrors of sex, which she did not want him to know anything about. Joe, as though he were much, much older than they were and was looking at them from a distance of so many years they appeared to him to belong to another generation, another world, thought, God preserve them. When, on Larissa's instructions, they became active, they did in ways that again seemed to leave Joe apart. Larissa went out of the room and Yura straightened the jerry-built table before the sofa, then went out of the room, too, and came back with mismatched plates and glasses and knives and forks and set the table. From the wardrobe he took a bottle of wine and opened it. In a short while, Larissa came in with a big, dented cooking pot, which she held out before her with a rag about the long handle. Only when everything was ready did they call Joe over to the table, where, Larissa side by side with Yura on the sofa and Joe on a wooden chair, they ate boiled fish and potatoes and drank wine.

Yura and Larissa talked between themselves, she talking more than he, often throwing long strands of hair from her face. Sometimes the boy and the girl stopped talking and studied Joe. Yura moved slowly; Larissa quickly. She said *nyet* again and again, presumably disagreeing with Yura, then she frowned when she pursed her lips to think. When Yura spoke, she held out her hand to stop him from thinking. Then the idea came to her, and shaking her head and at the same time throwing her hair about with her hands, she spoke seriously to Yura. He said, *"Da."*

They both stood in the small space beyond the table, and bending over from their waists so their backs were straight, they took off their shoes, hers scruffed pumps, his large old man's shoes with worn heels, and while Larissa called out commands to him, Yura held her in his arms and she leaned far back so her hair fell, then he swung her from one side to the other and lifted her so she was lying across his arms, then he lifted her up high over his head and she raised a leg and touched the knee of the other leg with her pointed toes, and for a moment they remained still. That pang came to Joe again with a sudden rush of tears to his eyes. When Yura lowered Larissa, with slow gentleness, to the floor, the two young people smiled at one another. Joe clapped and they bowed.

Looking at them, Joe all at once thought, But I love Zoya. He asked, *"Zoya, gde?"*

Larissa jumped as she grabbed Joe's hand and, speaking fast in Russian, pulled at him, so he rose. She put on her shoes and Yura did his, and then she continued to pull at Joe across the room and out into the hallway to their coats hanging on hooks, and as she and Yura put on their coats and hats, so did he.

They took him down into the metro, changing stations from time to time to run to trains on other lines, and they came up near the Bolshoi Opera House. Larissa took one of Joe's hands and Yura the other to rush him along to the side of the Opera House and in through a battered side door.

Just inside, a group of old people were gathered about the doorway of a small anteroom. In the anteroom, a man sat at a small, rickety table. He wore felt boots and a coat. The old women in the group wore knitted caps. They glanced at Larissa, leading Joe, followed by Yura, who passed them, but they glanced expressionlessly. If they had originally stood guard to stop people from entering, they no longer cared who did enter.

At the garderobe, the three took off their coats, hats, gloves, and passed them across a counter to a woman with a knitted cap who said nothing to them.

Yura and Larissa, whispering to one another in Russian and sometimes laughing, took Joe to the very top of the opera house. As they walked along a curving corridor that followed the curve of the cupola, Larissa put her finger to her lips to indicate they must be quiet. Along the corridor were practice rooms—with КАБІНЕТ painted on the closed doors—from which, as they passed, Joe heard a woman singing, or a piano playing. The old, springing parquet floor creaked under their feet, and Larissa kept her finger to her lips as though that would stop the floor from creaking. The smell, a smell that got into Joe's sinuses and burned a little, was the dust of the old opera house.

Then, pressing her finger more emphatically to her lips, Larissa led Joe, always followed by Yura, through a narrow doorway and along a narrow gangway to the top balcony of

the house, high up under the painted ceiling with its chandelier. There were people in these high balcony seats like shadows. Joe leaned over the heads of these shadows to see, far
below, the illuminated stage, and an old woman in a chair singing with great grief, her voice resonant when she sang those
low, long Russian notes though she was in fact singing in
French with a refrain of *"Je ne sais pas pourquoi,"* notes that
were the lament of her deep grief.

The singer finished her aria, and Larissa touched Joe to let
him know they must go, and the three tiptoed out and went
down, down, down stairs, from level to level. Joe could hear,
in the distance, muffled music. They went into the empty foyer
of the opera house, its highly waxed floor gleaming, reflecting
the crystal prisms of the chandelier above. They stood still and
listened to the distant Russian music.

By a narrow door, they went along more curving corridors,
through doorways into more curving corridors that took them
backstage, and no one stopped them. The backstage corridors
were covered with old linoleum over the old parquet, and the
walls were painted thickly with green, glossy paint. At intervals
along the walls were plastic loudspeakers over which the per-
formances on the stage sounded very far, with static. In a corner were copper kettledrums and a small harpsichord covered
in a torn black rubber sheet. Larissa pressed her finger even
harder against her lips as she rushed ahead, and Yura rushed,
too, to join Larissa, as though where they were going now
needed both the young people to bring Joe there. They appeared to be a little frightened of what they were risking. They
passed through a doorway with a thick, battered, metal door,
then they climbed metal stairs past a low, dark room with its
metal door open, inside of which were great black pulleys and
ropes. Joe, looking to the right and left and not ahead to where

the children were hurrying, found himself, when he did look ahead, on the side of the stage of the Bolshoi. He saw, between the flats of a pastoral scene, onto the stage center, where, in light so bright it appeared to make them glow silver, were two singers, a man and a woman, facing an audience Joe couldn't see, and singing, in Russian, an aria that rose and rose with their love for one another.

On the other side of the stage, between flats, Joe saw Zoya. Joe's immediate impulse was to walk across the stage to her, an impulse so strong he had to hold himself back from it. He listened to the end of the aria, then the clapping.

Zoya came to him from behind and put her arms around him, and Joe felt all his body give way to her, so that for a moment before he drew back she was holding him up. He kept hold of her hand.

In the buffet of the opera house, Zoya and Joe sat side by side holding hands while Larissa talked to Yura in nonstop, rapid Russian, admonishing him, maybe even reprimanding him, about something, while he simply listened. Only from time to time did he turn his eyes, which, with the slight Asiatic folds at the corners, appeared to look at someone at a distance, to Joe, and he smiled at Joe, though his smile, too, seemed to be at someone at a far distance. Joe held Zoya's hand more tightly and smiled back at Yura.

"What is she telling him?" Joe asked Zoya.

"She is advising him about his future."

"What future?"

"They are both passionate about ballet and want to dance at Bolshoi, but Bolshoi, like everything in our country, is going down, and soon it will only survive because of tourists paying to see what was once great and they think is still great because it once was."

"So what is she advising him?"

"That he must leave Russia and go to ballet school in the West."

"And what about her?"

"She is more concerned about him than herself. She believes he is a great dancer."

"She loves him."

"Yes, she loves him."

Joe studied the young couple, Yura intent on what Larissa was so intently telling him. "And he loves her."

"He loves her," Zoya repeated.

All along the walls, in niches, were porcelain Russian vases with pastoral scenes on them, and behind the bar of the buffet were glassed-in cases with crystal vases and bowls. Among the people waiting in the line at the bar was a group of young ballet dancers, girls, in their practice clothes, their hair severely pulled back into small, tight knots held by gold or silver nets, their smooth, long, thin napes visible down to the vertebrae when they leaned toward one another. With their coffees and plates of biscuits, they went to a table across the room, and Joe, listening to Zoya and Yura and Larissa talk, continued to watch them all the while they sipped at their coffee and nibbled their biscuits.

Zoya said, "I have told you so much, why not tell you more? When I worked for KGB, I was assigned to watch the dancers of Bolshoi and their relationships with foreigners. There is behind Bolshoi Theater a big building that used to be headquarters for KGB especially watching Bolshoi artists and their relationships with foreigners. I used to come often to Bolshoi and bring Yura with me, so, since he was child, he has been passionate about ballet. Everyone here knew me, and everyone knew why I came, and everyone here was very attentive to me and to Yura because of me. I still come, and everyone knows I come now only for myself, come because I love to be here, come because I, too, still think it is great because it was once so great, but everyone is used to me and they let me come. Years ago, when it truly was great, Yura asked me if he could study dancing, and I asked and I was told, of course, of course. No one would want to deny me the privilege of his studying ballet. You do not know how strange it is to have authority. You never think you are abusing it, you think you are asking something of friends and your friends are very obliging. They say, 'Of course, of course, with pleasure,' and you think how agreeable they all are, how much they like you and Yura. Yura does not know this. He is, in fact, a very good dancer. Maybe not great, as Larissa thinks, but good. But he is no longer a privileged person because I am not. Some people in KGB were able to keep their privileges even though they ceased to be KGB. Some transformed their privileges very much to their advantage, but I have lost all my good privileges except that no one minds if I come and wander around Bolshoi."

"You've known Yura since he was a child?" Joe asked.

"Yura is my son."

"Does Gerald know that?"

"No." As though Yura and Larissa could understand English, Zoya said something to them in Russian that made them stand, but before they left Yura said something to Joe in Russian that Joe asked Zoya to translate.

Zoya said, "He wants to ask you something in the little English he has learned."

Joe said to the boy, "Ask me, Yura."

Enunciating carefully and gravely, Yura asked, "Please, do you have hope for Russia?"

Startled, the sudden impulse came to Joe to cry out and reach for Yura's head and press it to his chest.

Yura's calm but sad eyes were fixed on Joe.

Joe's breath heaved, and he had to wait a moment before he said, "I have great hope for Russia."

Yura bowed his head a little and said, "Thank you."

Then Zoya said something to her son, who approached Joe closely and kissed him three times on his cheeks. Larissa followed Yura, and the young couple went off together, Larissa, perhaps, insisting on knowing what Yura had asked Joe and what Joe had answered and commenting on the exchange.

"They are too beautiful," Joe said.

"Please do not say that," Zoya said.

"I'm sorry."

"The last thing I want is for Gerald to know that Yura's my son. Did you see him in the apartment?"

"I saw him."

"Was he drunk?"

"He was getting drunk."

"I will wait until he is very drunk, then he will not remember if I came to see him or not. Did you tell him you saw me at the National?"

"Yes. He asked me if you were working."

"And you said?"

"I said I supposed that you were working."

"I was working."

"Do you know what happens to the girls once they get to other countries?"

Zoya stared at him flatly.

"Why are you doing this? So Gerald will marry you and bring you to America? You want to go so much?"

"For myself, yes, but for Yura more."

"So that he will become a ballet dancer?"

"So that he will become something. He will become nothing here. I worry, I worry so much what will happen to him if our country falls apart more and more. Will there be wars on all sides, wars with all the republics that break away, and will Yura have to fight to keep them in the Union? Can you imagine what it is like to be a soldier in Soviet army even now? I know mothers who try to get their sons admitted into insane asylums, because in the insane asylums the conditions are better than in Soviet army. In Soviet army, each soldier has one spoon to eat with, and after he eats he licks the spoon and puts it in his boot. That is only one aspect of army life that may be funny, but it shows how bad everything is. I won't have it, I won't have it."

"Does Yura know you want to get him out?"

"No."

"Would he leave Larissa?"

"He would have to. I cannot save everyone."

"But supposing he wouldn't leave Larissa?"

"Don't ask such questions."

Joe watched the young ballerinas at a table across the room get up, all together, their backs straight, their gestures slow and simple and pure, and walk among the empty tables and out.

He had come to tell Zoya not to go to Gerald, had come to tell her never to go to Gerald, had come to tell her that Gerald would never marry her; but to tell her about Gerald, all of that, everything about Gerald, seemed to Joe of a flatter banality than ever, and he thought there was no point in telling Zoya anything because none of it was interesting.

Whatever Gerald was capable of imagining, all he was capable of doing was to get drunker and drunker, to rave more and more crazily in his alcoholism, and to become helpless. He wouldn't marry Zoya, and he wouldn't do anything he fantasized doing to her, because, finally, Gerald would not be able to do anything, and Zoya would be left with a big man lying unmovable in a puddle of his vomit. And this, too, Joe found too banal, too uninteresting, to warn Zoya about. Zoya should have known, and maybe Zoya did know, but even her desperate attempt at not knowing, at continuing to believe that Gerald would marry her so she would be able to get herself and Yura to America, roused nothing more in Joe than a sense of fatigue about Zoya. Her relationship with Gerald did not concern him and he didn't want it to concern him.

And yet he asked, "Has Gerald ever been to your apartment?"

"No."

Joe tried to smile. "You were too ashamed to let him see it?"

"I was too ashamed."

"Where does he live?"

"He lives in National Hotel."

"And where did you meet him?"

"I met him at Bolshoi, during an interval of a ballet, in the foyer. I was alone, as I often was when I went to performance at Bolshoi, and he came and talked to me. Maybe he thought I was a prostitute. He was a handsome man just three years ago, buying, he said, works of Russian art for commercial galleries in the West, which was just beginning to be a possibility then, a possibility we thought of as glasnost and not yet as a collapse. And he knew everyone in all the big embassies, was invited to all the embassy parties because he made everyone, even Soviet officials, laugh. He would make jokes about their rows of medals, and they, amazingly, would laugh. And sometimes I was his guest. I thought he must be working for American intelligence."

"Was he?"

"I do not know. All foreigners in Russia are thought to be working for intelligence."

"Even I?"

"I don't think you."

"I don't look as though I could be?"

"No, you do not look as though you could be."

"You know he's not a good man, but you'll see Gerald again?"

"Please do not ask me these questions, Joe. You are asking too many questions I can't answer."

"You will?"

She dropped her fists into her lap and sat up stiffly. "Yes, I will."

Joe's hat was on a chair next to him, his coat draped over the back. He picked up his hat and put it on.

"You're going?" Zoya asked, her eyes wide and staring.

"Yes." Joe stood and began to put on his coat.

"Will you see me again?"

"Maybe not."

Zoya's body slumped as she fell against the chair back, and Joe saw in the slump her total resignation, a resignation that she must have had to accept over and over and would have to go on accepting over and over. She said calmly, "I do not blame you."

"No."

"I am sorry for Yura. He likes you so much."

"I like him."

"Maybe you would see Yura?"

"I don't think so."

"Will you tell me some expression in English I will tell him? He likes to learn expressions in English, even if he doesn't understand what he is saying and I have to explain to him again and again."

"I can't think of anything original now."

"I understand." Still slumped back, Zoya ran her fingers through her hair as if to try to arrange it. "What will you do now?"

Joe raised his shoulders and let them drop.

"Go back to America, Joe."

"I'll think about it."

"Now, you will return to apartment?"

"Now, yes."

"And if Gerald is there?"

"Is there something you want me to tell Gerald?"

"No, nothing."

As Joe was turning away, he turned back and asked, "Aren't there other ways of getting to America than to marry Gerald? Many Russians do go, you know, many, so parts of New York, like Brighton Beach, are Russian colonies."

"I counted on Gerald."

"I see."

"Don't turn away from me without giving me a kiss."

Joe went to her and, leaning toward her, saw her white face, which appeared not beautiful but gaunt. She reached for his shoulders to pull him down to her, and as she did, he felt, more forcefully than he had ever felt before, a pull to give in to something, a pull that seemed to him to wrap round his body like tight ropes and yank at him, and a terror passed through him. He jumped back from her.

With a fine wail, she asked, "Am I so evil to you?"

He stood still and breathed in and out, and after a moment he again leaned toward her and kissed her on the cheeks, three times, on her right cheek, on her left cheek, and again on her right cheek, as he knew Russians did. Then he turned away.

He could not find the key to the apartment in his pockets, though he knew it was there. He hoped that when he rang the bell, no one would answer, and though he had no idea where he would go, he would go back out.

An almost unbearable heaviness came over him when Gerald opened the door, Gerald without his jacket, his polo shirt stained under the armpits and the collar stretched so far down his white, greasy chest showed. He was carrying the bottle, which was still more than half-full.

With a scowl, Gerald asked, "Who are you?"

"I'm Joe."

That was enough for Gerald to turn back into the apartment, staggering so he fell against and bounded back from walls, and let Joe follow him. The air was fetid.

"I've been waiting for Zoya," Gerald said.

"She didn't come?"

"No, unless she came and I've forgotten, which is very possible."

"She didn't come with a prostitute for you to have a look at her?"

"I think I would have remembered that." Gerald sat monstrously in an armchair and placed the bottle against his fly. "Not that I remember much."

"You don't remember the interesting conversation we were having before I went out?" Joe asked, taking off his hat and coat and sitting, as if he had never left it, on the sofa among the messy bedclothes.

Gerald frowned so deeply, his eyebrows beetled out over his eyes and almost covered them. "What were we talking about?"

"We were talking about Zoya."

"What were we saying about Zoya?"

"You were saying."

"Was I? Well, I know a lot more about Zoya's life than she thinks I know."

"How? Through the KGB or the Mafia?"

Gerald laughed one of his short, abrupt laughs.

On a sudden impulse, Joe asked, "Do you know her son?"

Gerald became motionless so as not to let on in any way that he didn't know. "I know him, I know him. What's his name?"

"Yura."

"That's right, Yura."

"He has a girlfriend called Larissa."

"That's right, Larissa." Gerald tried to raise his heavy, beetling eyebrows by opening his eyes wide a number of times, but they kept falling as if of their own bushy weight. "I know about Yura and Larissa."

A sweat broke out all over Joe's body.

"What was I saying about Zoya?" Gerald asked.

"How much you love her and want to help her."

"Oh, yes, I love Zoya and want to help her."

"And her son, Yura, and Yura's girlfriend, Larissa."

"I want to help them all."

Joe felt the sweat run down his body.

Gerald said, "I couldn't find a glass to drink from, so have been drinking, disgustingly like a hopeless alcoholic, from the bottle."

"I'll find you a glass." Joe went into the kitchen, where he stayed for a long moment, his hands over his face. He rinsed one of the little, etched vodka glasses, left dirty on a table, and went back to the living room with it.

"I was waiting."

Joe handed Gerald the glass without speaking, then huddled among the bedclothes.

Gerald filled the glass and drank it down, filled it again and drank it down, and filled it yet again and drank it down.

"Do you hate your imagination?" Gerald asked.

"I loathe it."

Gerald laughed in an abrupt way, as if he were burping, but it was a laugh of complicity. "Right on. . . . Why?"

Joe shrugged one shoulder.

"I can tell you why. Because everything you are able to imagine that you feel is true has already happened in fact in history, has been photographed in black and white, so you are left with nothing else to imagine that you feel is true. You loathe your imagination for not being able to be more true than history. Isn't that so?"

"Maybe."

"Maybe? Of course it's so. I know. I know it about myself because, though I am a horrible and therefore loathsome person, I am historically true. You know that, and that's why you listen to me. Isn't that true?"

Joe looked down.

"Look up at me," Gerald commanded.

Joe looked up.

Gerald said, "Do you want to know why I always wanted to come to Russia? Being as interested as you are in me, you might have asked yourself, 'Why did he come to Russia?' I'll tell you why I always wanted to come to Russia. I wanted to come to Russia because I knew everything I was ever capable of imagining that was true had already happened, in documented black and white, in Russia, because Russia was, is, and will be the country of the greatest suffering in the world, beyond anyone's imagination. I wanted to come because Russia has suffered, is suffering, and will go on, forever and ever, suffering. That's why I wanted to come here. Suffering does something to me, Joe, if that's your name. It always has. It fills me with a feeling that is so strange, I can't begin to explain it to you, can't come anywhere near naming it. I don't mean my suffering, of course. I would do anything, and have done anything, not to suffer. No, suffering is not for me. I'm talking about the suffering of others, suffering beyond anything I could imagine, or endure. The closest I can come to saying what it is that the suffering of others fills me with is a sense of strange longing. You understand this, don't you? This is why I feel, deep down, that Russia in her suffering is a country of such great longing."

Joe closed his eyes.

Gerald said, "I can't explain the feeling, but I can say when it first occurred to me. Open your eyes—I can't talk to someone with his eyes closed—and I'll tell you."

Joe opened his eyes to see the big man in the darkening room.

The big man leaned forward and lifted the back of his jacket and took out from the back pocket of his trousers his wallet. "People usually carry photographs of their family in their wallets, but I don't have any family, or any that want to know me. They wouldn't care where I am or what I'm doing. In fact, I don't carry photographs of anyone I know." Gerald opened his wallet in a studied way and slowly flipped through the yellowish plastic holders in which Joe saw cards of different kinds, not only credit cards but, it appeared, old membership cards to clubs. Gerald slipped something out, looked at it himself and smiled, then, holding it up but turned toward him so Joe couldn't see it—all this done, Joe thought, for slow, dramatic effect—he said, "Look," and he turned the picture round to Joe.

At a distance, Joe saw only a gray blur, and he had to lean far over to see the picture clearly.

"This isn't a fake photograph. What it shows happened, wasn't imagined by anyone, was done in fact."

Joe rocked from side to side.

"I'll tell you where I first saw the photograph," Gerald said, as if not drunk but totally in control of himself, his eyes fixed, if not on Joe, on people around Joe to whom he displayed the photograph. "I saw it when I was a kid, in Washington, just after the Second World War. I was a kid but old enough to go through my father's desk when he wasn't home, when he was out being a senator. I was maybe sixteen. This was the time when the world was finding out what the Germans had been doing—doing in Greece, in Italy, in Poland, in Russia, never mind in Germany itself—and I found this photograph clipped to some papers in one of my father's drawers. I took it, took it and kept it in a drawer in my room where I had my secret collection of things, a squirrel skull and a prism from a chandelier and a golden tassel from a curtain and a little dagger with a mother-of-pearl handle, things that only I knew about and that I could look at whenever I wanted. I looked at this photograph a lot. I had never, ever seen anything like it." He held the photograph closer to Joe. "Take it."

Joe reached out for it, but looking at his hand reaching out, he dropped the hand. Gerald was still holding the photograph out to him.

"You never saw the photograph before?"

With a low moan, Joe said, "I did."

"She's Russian, this girl. She was a Russian partisan during the war. She was captured and tortured and hanged by the Germans. Her name was Zoya. Zoya Kosmodemyanskaya." Gerald turned the photograph round to look at it himself, and as if he were talking to himself, he said, "When I saw the photograph for the first time, I felt for the first time those feelings, those feelings from deep, deep down, those strange feelings roused by suffering, those feelings of such great possibility." He inserted the photograph carefully into his wallet and, raising his haunch, replaced his wallet in his back pocket. Then he said, looking at Joe, or around Joe, "What was the feeling I had? What? It was so strange, almost like love." Then he looked straight at Joe. "Shall I tell you what that strange sense roused in me by the photograph of Zoya inspired me to do?"

"No."

"You don't want to hear?"

"No."

"Sure, you want to hear."

"No."

"Shall I tell you, then, what you feel?"

"No."

"Then I'll tell you what you want to feel. You want to feel, looking at such a photograph, that there must be something beyond horror, something beyond the age of terror we all live in, don't you?" Gerald added severely when Joe didn't reply, "Don't you?"

Frowning so his eyes were almost closed, Joe, as if despite himself, nodded a little.

"And what could that be? Say, a sense of grief, the deepest possible grief, and beyond the grief the deepest possible love?" Gerald shouted, "Don't you want to believe that?"

Joe, nodding, kept his eyes down.

"And beyond love? What do you want to believe is beyond love? Redemption? You want to believe there is redemption for the age of terror we live in, don't you?"

Joe's nodding head went lower.

"And it could all happen, you want to believe, if only you could imagine something beyond all the horror."

Joe put his hands over his eyes.

"But you know you're wrong. You know that everything you want to believe can never be true, however much you want to believe in what you know is not true, don't you? Though you know you're bad, you want to believe you can be good, don't you? And though you know God doesn't exist, you want to believe that God does exist, don't you? Oh, Joe, you want so much, you want everything."

Joe dropped his hands, raised his head, and stood. He walked round the coffee table and Gerald in his armchair and down the room to the glass doors to the balcony. He stepped out into the snow and shut the door behind him. He shivered with the cold but he remained outside.

When he turned back, Gerald was gone.

FIFTEEN

The train station where the man got off was as far as the ticket he could afford took him. He had no other reason for getting off the train here. He went into the waiting room. A young woman was lying on the bare boards of the floor, her eyes closed, her hair spread out from her thin face. Standing over her, the man asked, "Are you all right?"

She opened her eyes to look up at him, but said nothing.

"Can you get up?"

Her breathing made her small breasts rise and fall, but she otherwise remained motionless.

"Can I help you get up?"

Her eyes were large in that thin, pale face, and staring. She appeared to be trying to communicate something to the man by her staring alone, as if she were dumb as well as unable to move.

The man crouched beside her, and when he did, her stare became more intent, her breathing more convulsive in a body she could not move. Her shoes were worn, the skirt of her dress dusty and wrinkled, and her dress altogether too big for her.

"Can't I help you?" the man asked.

He thought he saw her roll her head a little from side to side to let him know that he could do nothing for her.

A little wail rose from her when two men entered the station waiting room. She turned her head away from them and closed her eyes. The man stood back when the men came for her and, both reaching down at the same time, raised her to her feet. Her head lowered, her hair hanging over her face, she was held up between the men, and she staggered when they forced her to step forward, out of the waiting room.

The man would not try to imagine what had happened to her, or what would happen to her.

He waited, then left the station to walk along a road that led to a village. A group of people were gathered around the church, and he went toward them. They were looking up at the top of the church tower, where men, using a contraption of beams, pulleys, and ropes, were detaching the bell. As it was moved, the bell made a strange sound, like a low, moaning lament. The men swung the bell to the edge of the belfry, then out from the belfry into space, and they shouted to the people gathered below to move back before one of the men let the bell fall. It seemed to cry as it fell, and the sound it made when it hit the earth was like no other sound the man had ever heard.

He stood among the dispersing crowd. He didn't know where now he could go and what he could do.

SIXTEEN

Zoya came quietly into the apartment, as though taking a chance that there might be someone there she didn't want to see her and whom she would turn away from quickly before he saw her. She found Joe, lying flat on his face on the small Turkish rug on the parquet floor, his arms outstretched, and surrounded by hundreds and hundreds of red ruble banknotes. For a moment, she wondered if Joe was alive, he lay so still. Then she saw sweat running down the side of his face and the back of his neck and saw his pulse beating in his temple. She crouched low and called softly, "Joe?"

He opened his eyes to see her worn-out, wet boots, with the fake leather peeling off the heels. Then he turned over onto his side.

She said, "I know you don't want to see me anymore."

"You came looking for Gerald?"

"Yes."

"You thought I'd have gone?"

"Yes. No. I don't know what I thought."

She looked at the circle of scattered ruble notes, picked one up and studied it, and let it drop.

Rising on an elbow, Joe said with a high laugh, "I changed all my American money for rubles."

"All?"

There was a frightening hilarity in his voice. "All of it."

Frowning with concern, Zoya asked, "Did you get the form that allows you to turn rubles back into dollars?"

"I don't know. I don't think I got any form. But I'm not going to turn the rubles back into dollars. I'm going to spend them."

"On what, Joe? There is nothing to buy in rubles. You can only buy with hard currency."

"Then I'll just give all my rubles away."

"Joe." Zoya knelt by Joe, in the midst of the money, and looking into his feverish face, she said shyly, "I know you didn't want to see me again. I came thinking Gerald would be here. I came to tell Gerald something."

Again Joe said, "And you thought I would have gone?"

"I do not know, Joe, I do not know. Maybe I hoped you would be gone, maybe I hoped you would still be here."

"But, really, you came to tell Gerald something?"

"Yes."

"Gerald left, I can't remember when, and he didn't say if he'd be back or not."

Zoya put her hand on Joe's forehead. "Your fever is worse."

"It is."

"You need care."

Joe laughed his high laugh of frightening hilarity.

Zoya then picked up in both hands wads of rubles. "You must not give all this money away."

"If I can't buy anything with it, what else am I going to do with it?"

"Joe," Zoya said, softly admonishing him to try to bring him down from that high and frightening level of hilarity.

He sat up and picked up handfuls of the notes and piled them onto those she already held in her hands. "You take it all."

She dropped everything. "No."

"I changed five thousand dollars in traveler's checks into rubles and some greenbacks."

"Joe, you could not."

"I did."

"In black market?"

"I don't know what it was. Black, red, white. I went out with my suitcase and my money belt, I went out thinking I would find a hotel, but I went to the National, the Rossia, the Intourist Hotel, and there was not a room available, not for me, because I hadn't reserved from abroad. For a foreigner here, everything has to be done from abroad. As I was wandering around, wondering what to do next, a man stopped me and asked me if I wanted to change currency into rubles at a good rate, and I said yes. He took me to some small, grim, dim place. I signed all my checks and gave him all my greenbacks, everything I had in my money belt. He treated me very well, even gave me a glass of vodka, which, when I got out again, I threw up."

"That was illegal of him. Also, you took chance. He could have been KGB agent."

"If he was a KGB agent, he was very excited about our illegal transaction. He gave me so much money, in stacks, I had to get rid of some clothes from my suitcase to make room for them. We were both laughing. And I came back here, because I didn't know where else to go, to think what to do."

"I should not have let you leave me."

"You couldn't have kept me."

Looking away, Zoya said, "No, I couldn't have kept you."

"Now I've got all these rubles and I've got to decide what do to with them."

"Without the right form, you will not be able to change your rubles back into dollars."

"I don't want to."

"It is your fever that is making you do these things."

"You tell me what to do with all my rubles, if you think they're worthless. Shall I open the window and throw them all out into the snow?"

"Why did you do it?"

"Because I wanted not to be able to leave Russia."

Zoya began, slowly, to pick up the red notes and arrange them into piles.

Joe said, "No one understands how I love this country. I do, I love this country. I love this country, and I want to stay and stay and stay, and never, ever leave."

Arranging the money in neat stacks in a row on the floor, Zoya asked, "To do what, Joe?"

"To be Russian."

"And what do you think it is to be Russian?"

Joe lay back flat on the floor.

Zoya brought the piles of money to the desk, where they formed a red block.

Standing over Joe, she said, "Maybe I will tell you what I came to tell Gerald."

"I don't want to hear."

"Well, you are right, because you have every reason to mistrust what I have to say. You have seen in me a Russia that you have every reason to mistrust."

"But there is another Russia."

Zoya sat in an armchair, and looking down at Joe lying on the floor, she cried, "Another Russia?"

"There is."

Placing her elbows on her knees, Zoya leaned forward and pressed her hands against her face.

Joe didn't move.

When Zoya got up, she walked about, swinging her arms and body loosely, as though beside herself with all her feelings. "Well, I'd better go find Gerald and tell him what I have to tell him."

Joe sat up. "You can't go to Gerald."

"I must."

"You can't go alone."

"I have often seen Gerald on my own."

"You can't see him on your own now."

"What has happened that I can't see him on my own after I have so often seen him on my own?"

Joe, dizzy, had to sit still and again close his eyes for a moment. He stood. "If you have to see Gerald, I'll come with you."

Astonished, Zoya asked, "You think Gerald would do something bad to me if I were alone with him?"

"I'm coming with you."

"You are not well enough to come out."

"I'm not well enough to stay in."

"But if you do not want to see me, you want, less, to see Gerald and me together."

Joe passed his hands through his sweat-thick, black hair. "What you have to tell him, is it about your joint venture?"

Zoya looked away shyly. "It is."

"Let me tell you this. You think you know Gerald. You don't know him. You don't know what Gerald is capable of doing."

"I know."

"You know what he is capable of doing to you?"

Zoya pressed her lips together hard, then said, "I know."

"And you go on working with him?"

Zoya pressed her lips harder together and said nothing.

"No, you don't know Gerald, don't know what he's capable of, don't know what he's capable of doing to you. If you have to see him, I'm coming with you."

"To guard me against him?"

"Maybe."

"Maybe you should hear what I have to say to Gerald. Yes, come with me to National."

Zoya had to help Joe on with his coat, but once he was in it, he went to the desk and pushed stacks of rubles into all his pockets, into his trouser pockets, into the inside pocket of his jacket, the breast pocket, the hip pockets, and into the inside pockets and hip pockets of his overcoat.

"What are you doing?"

"I want to take all my money with me."

"You are crazy. Foreigners are beaten up in Moscow streets and robbed."

"That's all right."

Joe even pushed a wad of money into his shirt pocket, and as he did, he laughed with that hilarity that frightened Zoya.

"Maybe you should not come. You are not well at all."

"I'm coming, I'm coming."

But he stopped her as they were leaving the apartment. "Do

you know anything about a girl tortured and hanged by the Germans named Zoya Kosmodemyanskaya?"

"Of course I know about her. She is Soviet saint. She was a fanatic. She wanted to be tortured and murdered."

"That's impossible."

"It is very possible."

Joe turned away from her to face the wall of the small entrance hall.

"I was named after her."

Joe pressed his face against the wall.

"You will stay here. I will go tell Gerald what I have to tell him, and then, whether or not you want to see me, I will come back to take care of you."

"I'm coming."

Joe was just behind her when they went out into the snow.

"Now, without dollars, we will not be able to take taxi," Zoya said.

"We'll go by metro."

"Will you be able to make it?"

"I will."

They got out at Karl Marx Station and walked through the late-afternoon darkness and snow to the National, its glass doors lit up, and outside the parked cars and the prostitutes. Zoya stared straight ahead as she and Joe went among them, as if they did not exist for her. At the hotel door, there was no commissionaire either to stop them from going in or to open the door to them. Inside, Zoya went from the lobby up the carpeted stairs and down a dim corridor with rooms on either side, the carpet embedded with dust, the wallpaper on the walls loose at the seams, and water stains on the ceiling. At the end of a long corridor was a desk where, usually, the woman who would not let you into your room unless you had a pass to exchange for your key sat among seltzer bottles and teapots, but the desk was bare, as though no woman sat at it anymore and controlled who came or went. Zoya knocked on a door, and soon Gerald, in pajamas, answered.

His gray hair was disheveled and his pajamas were half-unbuttoned, revealing hairy parts of his body. He didn't say anything to Zoya and didn't even look at Joe, but turned back into his room and evidently meant them to follow him.

He stood, staggering a little in his drunkenness, in the middle of the room and said, "They don't make up my bed anymore or change those useless towels in the bathroom, or even clean. Do you think this is their way of getting me out because I haven't paid?" Staggering, he sat on the edge of his unmade bed. "I hope, Zoya, you've come with some money, some money from the powers that be for convincing some pretty girl to get out of this godforsaken country, so I can at least pay part of my hotel bill." He looked about, it suddenly occurring to him that he had forgotten something important. "Did anyone see a bottle of vodka?"

Zoya said, "It's on the floor at your feet."

Looking down, Gerald said, "Ah, there you are, right next to my big, ugly, bunioned feet." He almost fell over as he reached down for the bottle, but Zoya rushed to him to lift the bottle to him, and he took it and drank from it, then studied it. "It has a way of disappearing." Holding the bottle out to Zoya and Joe, he asked, "Will you have some?"

"No," Zoya said.

"And you?" Gerald asked Joe.

"No."

"No one can ever say I'm not generous with my liquor." Gerald swigged more, then asked Zoya, "Have you come with some money?"

"No."

"No?" Gerald appeared, not angry, but puzzled why Zoya had not brought money.

"I have to tell you, Gerald, I have other work now."

Apparently not hearing, Gerald said to Zoya, pointing the bottle at Joe, "Why did you bring him? Is he now in on our joint venture?"

"We no longer have joint venture, Gerald."

"No longer have joint venture?" Gerald asked as, still puzzled, he tried to understand.

"No, I have another job."

"What other job?"

"I have a job now at Bolshoi."

"At the Bolshoi? Everyone knows that the Bolshoi is now a joke. How can you have a job at the Bolshoi?"

"I will help with Bolshoi publications of picture books on the history of Bolshoi, on the history of dancers and singers."

"You mean, picture books to sell in the Bolshoi gift shop along with cheap souvenirs, like tin trays painted with flowers and ceramic eggs and hollow wooden dolls that fit into one another, so the Bolshoi will be able to finance itself when the state drops it."

"We must, now, finance ourselves."

"That kind of job is not going to get you anywhere, certainly not out of the Soviet Union to the United States."

"I know that."

"You can't mean you're giving up on getting out and coming to America with me?"

Zoya said in the strictest voice, "I am giving up our joint venture, Gerald."

Gerald smiled. "Well, I can't say you've been doing a whole lot lately to merit your being part of a joint venture with me."

"Not a whole lot."

Gerald stood and, hitching the bottoms of his pajamas about his large waist, began unsteadily to walk about the room. He seemed to be thinking, his puzzlement slowly, as he understood, giving way to anger.

He turned to Joe and shouted at Zoya, "So did you take him along to protect yourself from me?"

Zoya held her place, and behind her stood Joe, who thought he might vomit.

There was then a silence in the room, with Gerald listening to something he alone appeared to hear. "Just a minute." He went to the loudspeaker, hidden beneath a circle of black material, that was meant to be for radio broadcasts, the black switches for which were on the wall, and he leaned close to it to listen more intently. Voices of people having a conversation were coming faintly over the loudspeaker, and Gerald shouted into it, "You're supposed to be listening to us talk, you idiots, instead of us listening to you talk. You've got the surveillance system ass-backwards." A click sounded over the loudspeaker and the voices ceased. "That's what the KGB are up to now— instead of listening in on other people's conversations, they let the whole world listen in on theirs."

Gerald walked again about the room, from time to time taking swigs from the bottle, and when he was near a small table, he knocked it over with the swing of a fist and shouted at Zoya, "I'm not going to let you go."

This startled Zoya. "Gerald, I have brought you nothing, nothing, for a long time. You have always said you could find someone else easily, someone who would bring more in for you."

"Find someone else in the pathetic condition I'm in? Look

at me. I'm about to be thrown out of this hotel, and you know we only have the apartment because of the good graces of the powers that be for business use, and once they find out there is no business, as I'm sure they more than suspect now, that apartment will go, and where am I? Tell me that, where am I?"

"I don't know where you are, Gerald."

"I know what's happened to you. You're still indoctrinated by Party directives, even if you no longer belong to the Party. You follow the directives from above, which are that you should be self-sufficient. You know that self-sufficiency is an impossibility in Russia, always was, is, and always will be. You all need to be told just what to do by some higher authority, and you are all terrified by that authority. Your lives are regulated by bureaucracy, were regulated by bureaucracy long before Communism and will be regulated by bureaucracy long after Communism goes. You are oriental and can't be Western. You are used to despots. You would be lost without them. You even need them to tell you to be self-sufficient. So you are going to work to make the Bolshoi self-sufficient. That is funny. Just think of all Russians now trying to make themselves, because it is the latest directive, self-sufficient. Just think of the chaos. It will be very funny to watch. If you stayed with me, you'd find out, really find out, about self-sufficiency, which is bred into the bone of each and every American. You're trying to be what you can't be."

Joe, feeling weak, put his hand on Zoya's shoulders to lean a little against her.

"I was teaching you self-sufficiency," Gerald said, "and you have learnt nothing, nothing. I invested my whole being into teaching you self-sufficiency. And what do you do? You give up on me, who can teach you the real thing, and you take up something that is in no way real and will fail. And where do you leave me?"

Gerald's raving didn't make any sense to Joe, but with his fever nothing made sense. He heard voices without knowing what they were saying, though he did know that Gerald was demanding money from Zoya.

Joe said to Gerald, "I'll give you money."

"You?" Gerald said with a cracking laugh.

"I'll give you five thousand rubles."

"And how far will that get me?"

"You can pay your hotel bill."

"If the hotel will take rubles."

"It will," Zoya said.

A sudden bright redness flashed in Gerald's face, and his eyes, the whites also red, bulged, and as he stared at Zoya, a crazy look appeared in all that redness.

Zoya stepped back, and Joe with her, as though Gerald were going to approach them, but he remained where he was by the table knocked over onto its side, one of its legs broken.

In a low voice he said, "I love you, Zoya."

Now, his head lowered and his shoulders raised, his face dark red, he advanced toward Zoya. The vodka in the bottle he carried sloshed. He advanced slowly, heavily, his bloodshot eyes fixed on Zoya.

As he advanced, he said, breathing heavily, "I love you, Zoya. Believe me, I love you as no one has ever or will ever love you."

Zoya pressed up against Joe, who put his arms around her waist to hold her. Gerald, dropping the bottle, came within arm's reach of her, but his shoulders hunched, he kept his arms hanging low at his sides. All the muscles of his face appeared to sag as the color drained out of it, and his eyes, too, appeared to weigh down his face. The jacket of his pajamas was half-unbuttoned, and a large pink nipple showed in dense gray and greasy hair, and the pajama bottoms were turned so that the open fly revealed his thick, hairy thigh.

Zoya's face was twisted with fear.

Gerald said, "My suffering Zoya."

His body sagged more as he reached out to take Zoya into his arms. She jumped back against Joe, who drew her even farther back.

Gerald, his body sagging so he had difficulty moving, slowly turned away to go to his bed, on the way managing to pick up the sloshing bottle, and he slumped on the edge of his bed.

Hurriedly, Joe took out from his pockets wads of rubles, which he dropped to the floor.

Gerald roused himself to stand, and raging, he screamed, "Get out, get out, get out or I'll kill you."

Joe opened the door to the room and, his arms about her, brought Zoya out into the corridor. They hurried down the long, dim corridor, past the empty desk where a woman used to sit, to the top of the stairs down to the lobby. There, Zoya had to lean against a wall.

It was a while before she was able to walk down the stairs with Joe, who supported her. He straightened her hat, which had become crooked, and tightened her gray woolen scarf about her neck. They were walking to the Metro Station Prospekt Marxa when Zoya asked, "Did you give Gerald all your rubles?"

"Not all."

"At least not all. . . . You go home and get your suitcase and leave apartment for good. You will meet me later at Bolshoi, side entrance. I will take you to my apartment, which I am so ashamed of, but which I will not be ashamed of showing to you."

"You'll take me to your apartment?"

Standing outside the metro station, Zoya put her arms around Joe. "Please understand, I want nothing from you. I do not want you to take me out of Soviet Union, I do not want you to give me money, I do not even want that you should love me. Please understand."

"I understand."

"You will go to apartment and take your suitcase and meet me at Bolshoi?"

"I will."

"You will?"

"I will."

"Please do not do any strange things."

"Have I done anything strange?"

Her arms still about him, Zoya pressed her lips to Joe's face. "You are burning."

"Zoya, Zoya," he said, and laughed.

Now she pressed her lips against his open mouth, suddenly and hard, and as she did, he closed his lips to kiss her.

SEVENTEEN

He imagined being in the summer forest, picking ripe berries from bushes, with late sunlight slanting through the trees. When he would return to the cabin, he would find, set on the table covered by a white cloth embroidered in red at the edges, a bowl, a spoon, and a jug of milk. He'd fill the bowl with berries, then pour milk over them, and he'd stand at the window and watch the sun set through the forest as he ate the berries. With dusk, mist would begin to spread about the trees.

EIGHTEEN

HIS SUITCASE BUMPING AGAINST THE DOOR AS HE opened it, Joe went into the side entrance of the Bolshoi, where the same people he had seen before, all in felt boots, were in the same positions they had been in. They glanced at him and, expressionless, turned away. He put down his suitcase. His body felt sticky beneath his clothes, his hair matted beneath his hat, some of the black hairs of which dripped over his forehead.

The walls of the room appeared to begin to slant in different directions, and as Zoya, smiling, came to him, the floor appeared to slant toward her.

She said, "Now we will go to open market to buy food for big dinner. We will use rubles you have left."

"We'll use all of them."

"We will have big dinner with Yura and Larissa, and after you will stay in my apartment to get better."

Joe had transferred the rubles he had left, which were in stacks, from his bulging pockets into his suitcase, and when he and Zoya got to the open market, a large, pre-Revolution market with stone pillars and oriental arches, he put the case down in a corner, opened it, and took out handfuls of rubles, which he gave to Zoya. She said, laughing, "Enough, enough," and people passing, many with oriental casts to their faces and wearing embroidered skullcaps, stopped and laughed, showing gold teeth. "Enough."

Joe closed his suitcase, but didn't fasten it shut, so when he picked it up by the handle the top dropped open and his clothes, mingled with rubles, fell out.

Zoya piled his clothes, most of them dirty, all of them wrinkled, back into his case, shut it and secured it, and carried it herself through the market, along cracked marble counters on which were piles of lemons sprinkled with water, large bunches of fresh parsley and dill and mint, heaps of pomegranates, and great bunches of white and red grapes hanging from metal hooks above the counters. A man with an entirely oriental face held up a bunch of grapes to Zoya and Joe as they passed, and Zoya stopped to bargain with him and buy it. The man wrapped the bunch in newspaper, and Zoya put it into the suitcase, among the clothes. There were apples, heaps of cranberries, and small plums, and the dark hearts of sunflowers. There were counters piled with carrots and eggplants and cucumbers. Zoya stopped from time to time and bought from a man in an embroidered skullcap or a woman in a kerchief tied tightly about her head, all people from the eastern republics who flew into Moscow with suitcases filled with their fresh produce. On another counter were large, round pats of ricotta-like cheese, glass jars of sour cream, slabs of honey in the comb, and bottles of seed oil. There were hills of dried apricots and prunes and raisins. The vendors were all polite, calling out to Zoya and Joe to come taste their wares, holding out a bit of cheese or a slice of a pear on the blade of a knife. Zoya tasted, looked doubtful, discussed, bought. She was having a good time. In a separate section of the market were pork joints, beefsteaks, calves' heads, brains, whole piglets, great shanks of meat held out by vendors in white, bloodstained smocks for Zoya and Joe to come and see: lean meat, no fat, fresh. Zoya bought meat, bought flour, eggs, milk; and when the suitcase became too heavy for her, Joe insisted on carrying it. A lone girl in an embroidered, sleeveless jacket over a thick sweater was sitting before a large, clear-plastic bag of shelled walnuts, everything she had to sell. Zoya said, "Maybe I can make a walnut cake," and Joe said, "Buy them all, buy all her walnuts from her." Zoya, laughing, did, and the girl looked down at the rubles where the bag of walnuts had been. As they were leaving the market, Joe saw a flower stall of gladioli and chrysanthemums in tin cans, and he said, "We must have flowers," which Zoya bought and carried.

Zoya said, "We have spent, for some people, a year's salary."

"People who can't afford to buy here?"

"Only the very rich can buy here."

"I thought there weren't supposed to be rich and poor in the Soviet Union."

"You are still joking about our Soviet Union."

"Am I joking?"

They walked along the snow-covered sidewalk, Joe sometimes stopping to rest from the weight of his case. They passed the state-owned shops, with blue, stylized signs of what was sold inside—a loaf of bread, a bottle of milk, an apple—pasted on the dirty windows, through which Joe saw dark and static lines of people waiting at empty counters.

"They queue up," Zoya said, "in anticipation of a delivery."

"And if there isn't a delivery?"

"They go home without."

Laughing, Joe said, "Let me go into a shop and give away some rubles for them to go to the open market."

Zoya held him back by his arm. "They will think you are crazy."

They walked on to the metro.

Joe said, "But why is there food in the open market and not in the state shops?"

"I do not know."

"There must be a reason."

"I do not know."

Zoya, carrying the flowers across her arm, appeared to be happy.

She had to hold the flowers close to herself in the crowded metro, in which she and Joe stood in the midst of silent passengers. Hefting his case, Joe followed her, always in the midst of crowds, when they changed from one train to another along passageways that were like the tiled corridors of palaces with chandeliers hanging along their lengths. Out of the center of the city, the metro stations were stark. More and more people got off, until Joe and Zoya were alone in the wagon.

They climbed the cement stairs of the station into a vast dark sky through which snow was falling in great, slow swirls. Near the station were two glass-enclosed kiosks, at each a long line of huddled people. In one kiosk a woman in a white smock and knitted cap was selling apples, and in the other another woman in a white smock and knitted cap was selling pieces of red meat she picked up with a fork from a basin filled with bloody pieces and dropped onto a sheet of paper and wrapped. Zoya and Joe passed these kiosks and continued into the snow-filled darkness, to where, in the far distance, were the lights of apartment buildings. As they walked, the snow made great, windblown swirls about them that caught Joe's breath away so he had to stop.

"I will carry the case," Zoya said.

But Joe insisted on carrying it.

They arrived at the battered metal door of a cement apartment house that looked as if it had been started and abandoned years before. The corridors, with bare bulbs hanging from the ceiling on wires, were cinder block and covered with graffiti in chalk, and the metal doors to the apartments were scratched with graffiti. Joe saw, written in big letters in the midst of Cyrillic, I WANT TO BE HAPPY. The cement floor was wet from melting snow.

Zoya opened the door to her apartment.

She said to him before she turned on the light, "For years I was promised better apartment, for so many years."

A smell of gas was inside the apartment, and when Zoya switched on the overhead light it seemed to shine dully through gaseous air.

On either side of the small room, its cinder-block walls painted green, were what Joe had once known as davenports, with knitted blankets and pillows on them. At the far end of the room was a plywood partition. All there was on the walls was a reproduction of an icon of the gentle head of Jesus Christ that Zoya said she had bought from an old woman in a metro underpass.

She said, "All the money I could earn, I spent on Yura."

The apartment was hot.

Arranging the blankets and pillows on a davenport, Zoya said to Joe, "You will lie here. Get into your pajamas, and I will cover you. Then I will bring you a hot drink."

Zoya pulled Joe's pajamas out of his case, which she then took with her behind the plywood partition and into what must have been her kitchen. Joe undressed, put on his pajamas, and lay on the davenport. He felt hotter than the hot apartment, and the longing came to him to run out into the freezing cold air and snow. Zoya came back quickly with a glass of tea with honey and lemon, and she propped pillows behind his head so he could drink, then covered him.

"You don't have aspirins?" he asked.

"No, I'm sorry."

"That's all right."

The glass of tea was scalding, and Zoya helped Joe hold it so the tea wouldn't spill.

"You rest now, and I will prepare our dinner. You will have a good dinner, with Yura and Larissa to cheer you up, and when, tomorrow, you wake up, you will be well."

Joe smiled at her over the rim of the glass of steaming tea. "But does Yura live here?"

"He has his bed behind the partition."

"And he sleeps here every night?"

"Sometimes he sleeps at Alla's."

"He and Larissa," Joe asked, not knowing how to ask the question so it wouldn't sound banal, "are they . . . ?"

"Lovers?"

"I wondered."

"No, they are not. Yura would tell me if they were. They love one another, they love one another very much, more, maybe, than if they were spending nights in bed together."

"Their love is pure."

Zoya laughed. "I no longer know, Joe, if you are joking or not when you speak like that."

Laughing a little himself, Joe said, "I guess I'm not sure myself."

"I will go now into the kitchen and prepare for our feast."

"I don't know if I have too much appetite."

"You will eat, and then you will be well."

Zoya went out. Sometimes Joe felt drawn back a long, long distance from what he saw, and sometimes he felt he was brought up very close.

Zoya put her hand on his forehead and said, "The tea was good for you."

"I'm still thirsty."

"I will bring you more tea."

She helped him drink it.

He asked her, "Have you ever been lost in a forest?"

"I was once, yes. That was during the brief period I spent trying to live outside the world. I was with the people I knew, in the forest, collecting mushrooms. I got separated from them and I got lost. I thought I must go in the direction of the sun, and all the while I kept calling and calling. Hours passed, hours. Finally, one of our group heard me. He told me that if I'd have gone against the sun, I would have gone into four hundred kilometers of unbroken forest, with no houses, with no one."

"Is this when you were staying in the monastery?"

"Yes, then."

"Was it snowing in the forest?"

"No, it was not snowing. Why do you want to know if it was snowing?"

"I thought it might be snowing."

Again, Zoya put her hand on Joe's forehead and held it there a long while.

"You will be better," she said, "I know you will be better. I have prepared a roast, and we will have soup."

"I'm really not very hungry."

"You will eat. As soon as Yura and Larissa come, we will eat all together. They will give you appetite."

She went out again and Joe closed his eyes. Zoya woke him by setting up a narrow trestle table at the partition's end of the room, and he watched her cover the table in what looked like an old red velvet curtain and go out and come in and set the table with mismatched plates and cutlery and glasses.

She said, "Yura and Larissa must come soon, or our meal will be overcooked."

She went out and came back with a bottle of vodka and, laughing, said, "I bought this for Gerald but never gave it to him, and now I take it as mine. Maybe a little vodka would be good for you."

"I don't think so."

"No?"

"I'm very thirsty."

"I will bring you more tea with honey and lemon, and by then Yura and Larissa will be here."

Again, she helped him drink the tea.

He asked her, "Were you brought up with any religion?"

"No, none. My parents were proper atheists. They would be shocked by my revisionism if they were alive and knew that I now believe and pray."

"What do you pray for?"

"You must know. You once prayed, didn't you?"

"Yes."

Zoya appeared to him to become very small, then very large.

He said, "I once read of an ancient religion in the Russian forest in which the devout prayed to a dark hole in the earth."

"I have never heard that."

"Maybe I know more about Russia than you do."

"Maybe."

"I sometimes think I had an earlier life in Rus, in ancient Rus, and prayed in the forest to a hole in the earth. I was all alone. There was snow falling. I remember snow was falling. And one day, wandering, I got lost in the forest and couldn't find my way out, couldn't find my way out of the great, snow-bound pine forest."

"Drink tea."

He raised his head to drink.

Zoya asked, "But where are Yura and Larissa?"

"Maybe they stayed for a performance at the Bolshoi."

"That is possible. As bad as it is becoming, Bolshoi is still everything to them. But they said they would be here over an hour ago. And Yura was eager to see you, and so, too, was Larissa. They should have been here an hour ago."

"They'll come soon."

"Yes."

"You are a believer. Tell me what you believe in."

"Your fever makes you stranger and stranger, Joe. Maybe you are joking with me?"

"Maybe."

"Nothing remains of what you believed when you were a believer?"

"I think, nothing."

"No, not nothing."

"Then what do I believe in?" Joe asked.

"In what I believe in, too—in grief."

"Grief?"

"Because grief inspires everything that belief in God is supposed to inspire, and so rarely does. It inspires tenderness, devotion, and love. It inspires reconciliation. It inspires all the best feelings that human beings are supposed to have. And that is why I believe that God, who is tender and devoted and loving, grieves for us."

"But then, when the grief passes, all the worst feelings return, and God vanishes."

Zoya said, "All that has already happened in the world, what is happening right now in the world, what will happen forever in the world, all that suffering is enough to keep our grief always with us. Our grief is forever, our grief is for all eternity, like God."

"And do you pray to God?"

"Grieving is praying, and you grieve."

A cry rose from Joe.

Zoya put the empty glass by the bed and lay down next to Joe and pressed her face against the side of his hot and sweating face.

He kissed her cheek, her temple, and when he tried to kiss her lips, she, sighing, drew away from him and sat up on the edge of the bed. She said, "I am worried now that Yura and Larissa have not come."

"They'll be here any minute."

Zoya began to pull at her hair. "I do not know, I do not know."

"They will be." Joe reached out to try to bring her back down beside him on the davenport.

But Zoya stood away from Joe and looked down at him. "Did you tell Gerald that Yura is my son?"

She went into such a far distance she seemed to Joe to disappear, and then she came so close he could see into the pupils of her eyes.

"Does he know about Yura?" she asked.

Joe saw, through her eyes, into a vast space, in which the walls of a house appeared to be coming together and drawing apart again and again in different ways.

Zoya said, "Maybe I should go to American embassy for a doctor for you."

"No, no, don't go to the American embassy."

"You are not well, Joe."

"Don't worry about me."

Zoya paced, pulling at her hair. "I am so worried about Yura."

A knock on the apartment door made Zoya rush to it as though the room were suddenly very big and it took her a long time to reach it, and when she opened the door, a young man stood outside at an even greater distance, but the blue envelope the boy handed Zoya appeared to be so large it filled all the space of the big room. Zoya shut the door and tore open the envelope and took out a shiny, black-and-white photograph, and as she held it up, Joe saw on it the blurred faces of a boy and a girl, their eyes wide, staring out in a flash of terror.

Zoya screamed and fell sideways to the floor. She kept screaming, holding the photograph in one hand as she crawled, sideways on her hip, across the floor.

Joe jumped up and went to her and she grabbed at him and, screaming, pulled him down to the floor. Joe tried to hold her, but she kept twisting and turning in his arms, screaming. She was screaming in Russian.

"Zoya," Joe called, "Zoya."

She went still, and after a moment she rose to her feet and said, "I am going out to find them."

Zoya put on her old boots, tied them up, put on her scarf and old suede coat and hat of cat's fur, and without saying anything to Joe, she left the apartment.

Weak, Joe had not had time to put on his clothes to follow Zoya out. He threw himself on the davenport. He was shuddering, and he drew the blankets over himself, but his shuddering caused them to slip off.

He stopped shuddering and became calm and found himself walking up a flight of white wooden stairs, and on the landing at the top of the stairs he opened a door with a crystal knob. In rows on either side of the room were beds covered in white bedclothes, and people were sleeping in the beds. As Joe passed between the rows of beds, he knew that the people in them were recovering from illnesses that had almost killed them and that they would now be better than before the illnesses struck them. He saw a naked arm rise from the bedclothes of one bed and a nurse in a white uniform come quickly to hold the hand for a moment then gently place it under the covers.

At the other end of the room was a door with another crystal knob, which shone at points when Joe reached out for it. He stood for a long while with his hand on the knob, and then, slowly, he opened the door into a bedroom.

The bedroom was surrounded on all sides by windows, with white curtains that billowed out and were drawn in against the sills, and in the middle of the room was a large bed, a bed like a huge wooden sleigh, and on it a woman, naked, was kneeling, and kneeling behind her was a man, also naked, calmly braiding her long, thick hair. Joe, or whoever Joe was, walked by them slowly. The woman's breasts appeared tender, the nipples only a little more pink than the breasts, which shook a little as she moved her shoulders with the movement of the man braiding her hair. As Joe passed them, she looked at him, and though she smiled at him, tears were running down her face.

He crossed the room to the other side, to another door, this one a double, paneled door with a tracing of gilt about the panels, and when he turned back, he saw that the woman and the man were gone, but on the bed, in the midst of the rumpled sheets, was a comb. And fine, glistening hairs floated about on the currents of air through the room.

As he leaned against the double doors behind him, they opened, and facing them, he saw, near or far he couldn't tell, a mature woman dressing a boy in white, in his First Communion clothes, helping him on with his white shirt, his white tie, his white socks, his white kneesocks, his white knee-length trousers, his white shoes, his white jacket; and all the while around them were men and women, drinking cups of tea and talking among themselves, but admiring him, patting his head and shoulders. One old man drew the stem of a white carnation into the buttonhole of his lapel. On the faces of the woman helping him to dress and the people circling him, tears were running in fine streams.

Joe, or whoever he was, left the room with the boy in his First Communion clothes and his admirers, and opening another door, he found himself outside, in a backyard, where a girl was swinging on a swing under a grapevine. She had a large bow tied to her hair at the top of her head. Though tears were running down her face, she said with a smile that her family was going out to the country to pick apples, and would he like to come?

As she said this, wagons appeared, horse-drawn, wooden wagons, and he and she got into a wagon among children and adults, all laughing and joking with the bumps and rattling of the wagons over the dirt roads into the country, but all with tears running down their faces.

And when they arrived at the huge apple orchard, they were

met by a large, muscular, bald man wearing blue bib overalls, who, as much as he laughed, wiped tears from his face with his laborer's hands.

Everyone disappeared into the orchard. Joe, or whoever he was, climbed a ladder among the branches of a fruit-heavy tree to pick apples and felt the ladder sway. When he descended, it seemed to him that he was the only one in the orchard, that everyone else had gone.

But the girl with the bow in her hair appeared from behind a tree. He went toward her, half tripping on the windfalls in the high grass, and approaching her, he saw the tears now falling from her smooth, soft, smiling face down onto the flat bodice of her pinafore.

The girl disappeared into Joe's own tears. He looked around, and the apple orchard disappeared into his tears.

Joe saw Zoya in the room, crouched low, her arms between her raised knees, rocking back and forth and moaning. She was wearing her suede coat, unbuttoned, and her hat was on the floor beside her.

Joe called, "Zoya?"

She looked at him for a long time, and whether or not she knew who he was and why he was calling her, she got up and went to stand over him. Her face was white and her hair was ragged.

She held out a hand to him. Sweating and shivering with his fever and hallucinating so that he saw what wasn't there and didn't see what was there, he managed to get up and put on his trousers over his pajamas, his shirt, his socks and shoes. He put on his overcoat and gloves and hat. She buttoned her coat and put on her hat and opened the door for him.

At moments he was pressed close to her packed in among people in a moving metro carriage; at moments he followed her along underground passageways with chandeliers; at moments he waited in the corner of a cold, dimly lit building that might have been a train station because porters were standing by luggage trolleys; at moments he stood with her on a station platform. And then they were on a crowded train.

Dawn rose through falling snow, a thin, gray light. They got out of the train in the middle of forest. The station was blue stucco, with white, neoclassical pillars supporting a pediment, and in the pediment a relief of double red bunting, and only one woman stood on the platform, wearing a visored cap and holding up a sign, which was a round, black dot surrounded by a margin of white. She lowered the sign and went into the station when the train left.

Joe followed Zoya round to the back of the station, where there were no footsteps in the snow. Their breaths caused great clouds to form about them that drifted away in the wind-driven snow as they went down a narrowing, snow-covered road into the forest, where they left the road to walk in the snow among the trees.

In the stillness and silence of the forest, the sudden cascade of snow down a pine tree, falling from branch to branch, startled for a moment, but the stillness and silence that returned was more profound than before.

As they trudged, the clear cold penetrated right through Joe's fever and made his thinking clear, so it was with great clarity that he thought there were people in the forest, invisible people who became visible only at instants in sudden, rising and falling whirls of snow among the dark trees. He and Zoya penetrated more deeply among these people, who gathered about them and followed them, an always greater and greater number, through clearings and into denser forest, where the drifts were so deep Joe and Zoya sank up to their knees and had to pull each other out. These invisible people, so many they swarmed about them in wide gusts of wind-driven snow that shook the trees, drew Joe and Zoya on. Zoya, panting, stopped, and Joe stopped with her, but he felt the ghosts of people encircling them to pull them as if with heavy ropes farther into the forest, there where they would themselves become ghosts.

Their breaths great clouds that almost hid them, they stopped before an immense drift in a hollow among the trees. Zoya's face was shining with sweat. She was looking starkly about at those ghosts pressing in on them, and when she turned to look at Joe in the same way, he put his arms about her, and slowly she put her arms about him.

As she drew him down into the drift, he thought he saw over her shoulder, through the trees of the forest, a steep-roofed, brown clapboard house with a fieldstone chimney entwined with a winter-bare tangle of honeysuckle.

ABOUT THE AUTHOR

DAVID PLANTE, who has lived more than half of his life in Europe, has published extensively: novels, articles, and short stories. He was the first Westerner to teach at the Gorky Institute of Literature in Moscow and was recently named Professor of Writing at Columbia University. He is a Guggenheim Fellow and an American Academy prizewinner, and a senior member of King's College, Cambridge.